IN THE
HANDS OF THE
FISHERMAN

IN THE
HANDS OF THE
FISHERMAN
A NOVEL

T. J. SWANSON

North Loop Press, Maitland, FL

North Loop Press
2301 Lucien Way #415
Maitland, FL 32751
407.339.4217
www.northlooppress.com

ISBN-13: 978-1-63505-357-9
LCCN: 2016914546

Printed in the United States of America

NORTHLOOP
PRESS

For Wendy

TABLE OF CONTENTS

PREFACE

My mom taught me to read when I was three years old. By the time I was eight, I had devoured The Yearling, Uncle Tom's Cabin, Moby Dick, and other hardcover books, while my friends were reading the *Dick and Jane* series and other primers. Mom and I loved to discuss the stories we read, and she had a simple approach to wisdom, frequently shared in the form of short but pertinent quips. While going through one of many difficult times in my life, one of Mom's pearls drifted into my thoughts: "God watches over drunks and cripples." That was the initial inspiration for this story. Whatever our convictions, none of us – especially the imperfect and infirm- want to go through life alone–and that description encompasses every soul that I have ever met. Thanks, Mom–for instilling in me the need for imagination, grace, and humility–among so many other things.

Although this story is based in real events, this is fiction and any similarities to people living or dead are entirely coincidental.

This story is dedicated to the ghosts of Little Lake Hanging Horn and the Luce Line Trail. And to Steve Carmazon, who took us out to the prairie on starlit winter nights, expanding our view of heaven.

PART ONE

DESOLATION
AND
RECOLLECTION

CHAPTER 1

The loud *THUMP!* of a closing car door resonated across the barren landscape. The sound didn't fit the setting as it shattered the frozen silence of the endless prairie. Just moments before, Bob and the car's driver had been listening to *The CBS Radio Mystery Theatre*. The creepy tale it told of murder, lust, and betrayal sent a shiver through Bob's body even before the harsh air of the cold January night had a chance to bite the exposed skin on his face. He looked out across the starlit plain.

"It can't be much above zero" he muttered to himself. The whispered words hung just outside his lips in a cloud of breath, then crystallized and sank slowly to the firm snow at his feet. Bob jabbed his ancient wooden skis into the windrow of plowed snow along the edge of the road and leaned his ski poles up against them. He stood quietly, letting his lungs get accustomed to the frigid air. His eyes followed the taillights of the car that had just dropped him off as they disappeared over the horizon. *Nice guy,* he thought. *Must think I'm pretty weird though, leaving me off like this, out here in the middle of nowhere.*

Bob's car had broken down in Cosmos, about forty miles east of where he was standing. He was sure that it was a frozen fuel line since, in his haste to get on the road, he had forgotten to use winter-blend diesel fuel in the old Mercedes that he had been driving for... well, about forever, it seemed. It had happened before. Several times in fact. No matter. He would just pick her up with his friends after they had finished the tour–hopefully in three to four days. He only hoped that nobody messed with the old girl. He smiled to himself. It didn't seem too threatening in Cosmos. Probably not too many carjackings.

His thoughts turned to his friends. The plan had been to rendezvous at this spot with Doug, John, and Bernie by 1:00 p.m. They would ski as far as they could before dark, then set up camp for the night. The thin lines heading east in the snow told him that they had obviously gotten here before him. A last–minute call from an old client requiring a building demolition estimate – well–appreciated during the slow season – kept him from driving out here with his friends.

Or so he had told them.

He had called Doug early this morning and told him that he would be no more than an hour behind them on the road, so they should wait for him at the beginning of the trail – until he got there. Doug had just laughed. That conversation had been a little over twelve hours ago.

"Always late," Bob snorted under his breath, "and they know it."

That's why John insisted that I carry the food for the second, third, and fourth day – if needed – in my pack, he thought with a frown, *the tents, cooking gear and food for the first day are in their packs.* His frown turned to a smile as he grudgingly nodded approval of their plan.

It's good to have friends who know you so well.

A very light breeze hit the back of his neck, sending another shiver down his spine.

"I'd better get going", he thought out loud as he looked east down the old railroad grade, straining his eyes to see if he could pick up any sign of life in the darkness.

Bob peeled off his goose down coat and stuffed it into his well–used and battered Gerry backpack. He opened another compartment, pulled out a Gore–Tex wind breaker and slipped it on.

―⌒◈⌒―

He had changed into most of his skiing clothes at the convenience store where the Mercedes was parked, having managed to nurse the lurching car into the parking lot. A helpful clerk spread the news that he needed a ride to the end (or was it the beginning?) of the Luce Line Trail near Gluek. Bob wondered, though, whether he would be better off hanging around and waiting until his friends got there? If the tour went as planned, they would be in Cosmos by tomorrow night anyway. Bob had been leaning toward staying in town – until a well–dressed older guy showed up. The chance to ride in the old man's cherry "62 Cadillac Coupe de Ville convertible was the deciding factor.

Besides, he thought, *I came to do the whole tour. I can't wimp out just because the car broke down. I'd never hear the end of it.* He didn't want to be razzed for the rest of his life.

All three of Bob's friends were very capable skiers, and in their prime were possible contenders for the U.S. Ski Team. Bernie was even a talented biathlete, but the peep sight on his Sako heavy barrel rifle had gotten knocked out of alignment on the way to the national tryouts and that, in turn, knocked him out of the competition. In the years that followed, other commitments kept him from trying again. That was a long time ago, but Bernie still talked about his brush with glory – after a Scotch or two.

No matter, Bob thought, stroking his beard. *I'm faster than they are. I always was.*

If it hadn't been for a strong dislike of conventional discipline, he might have made it to the Olympics. His coaches often told him so. He was always in the top five in the Central Division 15K and 30K races, and in the top ten in the 50k – and most of the time he was hung over when he competed. That was back in the good old days. Back when you slept in your car before a meet, and you couldn't take any kind of sponsorship if you competed at the amateur level. Back when Avery Brundage was in charge.

But it had all just been for fun, for Bob. He believed that most of the amateur athletes took themselves far too seriously, with way too much attitude. He'd rather live with the belief that he could be the best – if he really wanted to – instead of trying to prove it to the arrogant snobs. After all, when you're number one, everyone is out to get you. If you win, you're only first for a short time anyway. You can place second or third in every race and the bullies will never bother you.

He snapped on his old Landsem skis and tested his wax. Strong kick, lousy glide.

"Must be the snirt," he mumbled.

He knew that he had waxed his skis perfectly for the snow conditions back at the convenience store, but there was no wax for "snirt" – the mixture of snow and dirt found in windswept open fields that would frustrate even the best wax experts.

He slung on and adjusted his thirty-five-pound backpack, cinched down his pole straps, and headed down the railroad grade to meet his friends, his eyes still trying to adjust to the limited light. He had only gone about a hundred yards down the trail, when he stopped with a jolt. The old fella with the Caddy had dropped him off on the edge of Minnesota State Highway 277 where it intersected with the old railroad grade. There were distinctly three sets of ski tracks starting there, but, if they belonged to his friends, where was Doug's Explorer?

—◌✦◌—

The soft glow of a yard light at a distant farm-house cast a silhouette of an old abandoned shed about a quarter of a mile down the road, north of the trail.

Bob skied up the ditch alongside the road and found Doug's vehicle next to the shed with a moun-tain of snow piled all around it. It was the only place to park out of the way of the snowplows, and there was just enough room for one car. Now he was glad that his old car had frozen up back in Cosmos. Despite its obvious attributes, it was not all wheel drive and could easily get stuck in deep snow.

The relatively easy skiing down the edge of the plowed road was an inaccurate testament to the after-math of the blizzard that had hit the region only three days before.

"Storm of the Century", the old boy with the Cadillac had called it. He was a rather odd fellow, who never once asked Bob why he wanted to be dropped off with his skinny skis, after dark, on the side of the road. But he did talk about the storm. He said it was "God's way of slowing down folks – makes them stop to consider what's really important".

The old fellow never did say what he thought was "really important", but he had an infectious grin and a twinkle in his eyes that made Bob believe he was sincere.

Or crazy.

There was something about that look – and his mention of God – that reminded Bob of another man. He tried to remember who that was, but he couldn't dredge up the memory. And that car. There was some-thing familiar about that, too. Who in their right mind drives a classic convertible in the winter? Bob pon-dered this for a few seconds, then dismissed the thought as he skated off the road ditch and skied east down the trail again, hot air billowing from his mouth, instantly freezing to his beard.

It had been a calm day, so the wind hadn't blown snow over the tracks left by his friends. The vast bar-renness of the open plain made him feel small – a minute speck in a universe of black and soft gray. The sky, although clear, was moonless, allowing the pincushion of stars to pierce its velvety blackness– with almost maddening clarity – while simultaneously giving off very little light, making it hard to see his friends' tracks. At times he felt like he was being watched by a million microscopes peering down at him – scrutinizing and analyzing him, picking away at his soul. It made him shudder. He was better off looking at the trail and not watching the sky.

The old railroad grade was narrow out here, and his friends had had the advantage of skiing it in day-light. The top was windswept with only six inches of snow on it. This is where his friends had skied, but if you deviated from the path – as he did once when the sky closed in on him – you'd find the embankments along the elevated grade to be armpit deep.

"Snow drifts twenty feet high", the old man had told him with a wild look in his eyes and a nervous laugh. "Some of the folks out here were buried alive".

And, indeed, some were still shoveling out from it.

It was the blizzard itself that made this venture possible for Bob and his friends.

They had all skied parts of the Luce Line over the years, usually together, always in the stretch between Watertown and Plymouth. Along that stretch, there are tunnels and bridges – and trees that formed a canopy over most of the trail making it beckoning and beautiful, inviting you to see what mystery lies beyond the next curve. Not like here, where the prairie is open to the elements and there is no cover to shield you from the piercing gaze of looming stars, the relentless wind, and the blinding sunlight that even on the coldest day can leave your skin burned and cracked.

Out here, the weather's lack of mercy can be hauntingly exhilarating.

Bob and his friends had often talked about skiing the entire trail – all 115 miles of it – before they got too old to do it. But as with most plans people make, the years quickly passed and their plans and dreams became a distant memory. Work schedules needed to be kept, property needed to be maintained, and bosses and clients needed to be satisfied.

But a series of unexpected events, culminating with the blizzard, had created the window of opportunity for the four skiers to pursue this long–unrealized goal. A fire right before Christmas allowed John, and the other chemical engineers that worked with him, to take an extended holiday from their laboratory.

Doug and his girlfriend had spent the holidays – and most of January – in Jamaica for the last twelve years, but his girlfriend's mother had taken ill, so the doting daughter flew to Phoenix to take care of her ailing mom instead. Doug didn't get along very well with his potential mother-in-law, who always wanted to know why – after all these years – he hadn't married her daughter. Of course, in her mind, that was his fault. Doug thought it would be pointless to tell her that he had proposed "tying the knot" many times, but each time the response was "let's wait." His girlfriend kept pointing out that she had several friends who had gotten married after long engagements. Every marriage ended in divorce.

The painting contract that Bernie had scheduled got postponed at the last minute while the couple he was working for argued about the master bedroom colors – and of course that affected the colors of the hallways, great room, bathrooms, etc. Bernie dealt with this frequently, and his friends all said he should be nominated for sainthood for his patience. He'd just shrug his shoulders and say, in his deep Eeyore voice, "Oh well, it comes with the job."

The building demolition estimate that set the stage for Bob's tardiness had been a fluke. Normally he wasn't busy in the winter.

So when the "storm of the century" dumped over three feet of snow on the region, insuring that even the open areas would be snow – covered, the tour fell into place.

Bob's eyes were focused on the hypnotizing effect of the pulsing red lights of a radio tower that he had been skiing towards for the last twenty minutes. His thoughts wandered back to the man who gave him a ride. The fuzzy image of another man with the same laughing eyes and boyish grin slowly came to focus in his mind.

The recollection hit him like a brick. *Uncle Art! That's who it was! The man in the Cadillac reminds me of Uncle Art.* Bob's brain strained to recall more. *Jeez, he's been dead for….at least thirty years,* he thought. His mind dug deeper to try to remember more. It slowly came to him.

Uncle Art's father had built a log cabin on Lake Hanging Horn back in 1915.

Bob quickly did the math. *That was eighty-one years ago.*

Uncle Art's father – Great Grandpa Martin Christianson – had cut white pine logs off a family member's farm along the French River, upstream from Lake Superior, in the winter of 1914/1915, and hauled them to Lake Hanging Horn, near Barnum, with a team of horses to build the cabin. It had been a gathering place for family and friends for over fifty years until Great Grandpa died at the age of 94.When Great Grandpa passed on, the families were divided about what to do, so rather than squabble over it, they decided to sell the cabin. That was a very sad event in the family history.

Bob's thoughts drifted further back.

Uncle Art wasn't actually his uncle. He was his mother's uncle.

But everyone called him Uncle Art, he recalled.

He was oblivious to the snow crunching monot-onously under his skis. The rhythmic kick and glide motion that was propelling him closer to his friends was second nature to him. His body was fluid, having done this, tens of thousands of times before.

As his mind dug deeper, trying to remember, his pace unconsciously quickened.

As a young boy, I was scared to death of him. He frowned sadly, the ice in his beard crackling in protest to the unexpected movement of his jaw.

Oh sure, he had a beaming smile, soft blue eyes, and a kind, raspy voice, but it was that hump that caught your attention. Bob pictured an image of Uncle Art's grotesque form standing in the doorway of the log cabin after the darkness had made the woods around it an unholy place. The warm amber light glowing from the doorway seemed wrong. Instead of inviting you in, it made you want to run away – especially if you were a shy, chunky little boy.

Bob let out a deep sigh of shame, recalling his lack of compassion.

I was just a little kid, he muttered to himself, shaking off tears that were beginning to form at the base of his frosty eye sockets. He struggled to put the memory out of his mind, but despite his conscious effort, more images flowed back in.

The homemade wooden crutches with worn leather grips where the big man's large, gnarled hands grasped and masterfully controlled his conveyance.

The wide, green suspenders drawn tightly over the red flannel shirt on his broken back, holding up loose -fitting trousers that hung limply around his useless legs.

The massive arms and shoulders that kept him mobile. And that smell – the musty odor of an old man. Not repulsive, but not particularly appealing either.

Uncle Art had been dropped by his mother as a baby. An accident that had left him permanently crippled and had aged her way beyond her years. Bob never met his great grandmother, who died long before he was born. The one picture that he had seen of her, at the cabin, on the table next to Great Grandpa's bed, showed the face of a woman battered by grief and guilt. Even as a kid he thought that, if there was a picture to describe torment, that would be it.

How sad. How very sad. A hollow feeling came over him. He suddenly felt like he hadn't eaten in days. He gripped his ski poles and pushed off harder down the trail.

His steady pace was taking him to his first town of this long journey. The lights of Clara City just ahead of him seemed compressed by the darkness, as if the night didn't want the artificial illumination to escape. Clear, moonless winter nights are like that, especially out here on the open prairie. He crossed State Highway 23.

Looks like the town is boarded up for the night, he thought as his skis carried him down the back ways of the quiet burg – behind the stores, shops, and lumber yard that were serviced by the train that had run through here twice a day so many years ago.

—ᦒ🕸ᦒ—

The old Luce Line Electric Railroad discontinued service in 1967, the same year Great Grandpa Martin had died. It had taken another five years before the Chicago Northwestern Railroad Company pulled up the rails and ties – and, in 1976, the Minnesota Department of Natural Resources took it over and converted it to a multi – use recreational trail, eventually used mostly by horseback riders, bicyclists, and skiers east of Hutchinson. The section Bob was on, west of Hutchinson out to Gluek, was too desolate for most cross–country skiers, and undesirable to most bikers. Even the snowmobilers seldom rode on the trail – claiming it was too windswept. They preferred to ride the edges, where the snow got deep. But Bob and his friends were a hardy bunch, always looking for a new challenge. They had never lost their competitive spirit. Collectively, they knew that the most rewarding challenge was when you competed against yourself – and nature.

"Uncle Art loved to fish", Bob muttered under his breath. A thin smile broke the line of his frozen mustache as he thought back to one particular day from his childhood.

He chuckled at the memory of begging his dad to not make him go with Uncle Art, but, of course, his dad had said, "Ask your mother," and after that, he knew that he was doomed.

Dread often entered his mind when he was a pudgy eight-year-old. It was the fear of getting pushed around by bigger kids at school. The worry of having to play the piano in front of the whole family when they all got together. The horror of being laughed at by his older sister and her friends for crying when a movie had a sad ending (which wasn't fair, since when Old Yeller died, they cried too!). And then he had to go fishing with Uncle Art. At eight years old it seemed his life was getting harder all the time.

The recollection of that day made Bob's thin smile broaden until it reached the edges of his frozen beard. A couple of icicles at the edge of his mouth broke off and fell to the snow between his skis. He wiped his cold, wet nose with the back of his gloved hand.

A shadow darted across the trail in front of him and bounded across the frozen countryside. The animal seemed to float, eerily, above the ground, though Bob knew that it was apparently just too light to break through the firm crust of the windblown snow. His senses had been jarred back into reality by the sudden movement. "Nothing but a jackrabbit," he reassured himself through a whisper, "or maybe a fox." The light was too dim to get a good look as the apparition ran with great haste across the field to the south.

The texture of the snow out there was that of a white silk scarf laid gently across an unmade bed. The scene was inviting, captivating. *But don't let that fool you*, he thought suspiciously, *there's death in that soft, beautiful landscape*. Bob knew that, in a strong wind, those snowdrifts could gobble you up almost as fast as an avalanche on a mountainside. He had been buried in camp more than once, and windblown snow could be remarkably heavy, especially if it had particles of dirt in it. Over the years, he and his friends had lost a fair amount of camping equipment to the white stuff. He narrowed his eyes to address his surroundings. "The snow is a thief!" he yelled out loud. The velvety landscape seemed to look back at him innocently, taunting him.

The evening's exercise was starting to take its toll on his body. His lower back was sore and his shoulders were beginning to ache from the weight of his pack.

We should've done this trip ten years ago, he thought as he let himself glide to a stop. He took off the old Gerry backpack and set it in his skis.

"It's getting colder," he mused, "better have a drink."

A long swig of Scotch-flavored water satisfied his thirst. Yeah, his water had Scotch in it- just eight ounces or so per quart. "It keeps the water from freezing," he used to tell people – with a smile. It was a bad habit that went back as far as high school. Although he had always kept it from his coaches, he was sure they knew. How could they not smell it on him? He never made much effort to mask it. Back in those days, they cut you some slack. That was back when the term "zero tolerance" was only used when describing the workings of a nuclear reactor. Most coaches figured you were going to Vietnam in a couple of years anyway, so who were they to deny you your youthful foolishness before the insanity of that war took it away from you?

But, of course, foolishness becomes a crutch, then later a habit. Bob knew that it was his undisciplined behavior that had kept him from becoming a top athlete, years ago.

"No matter," he laughed, pulling the ice off his beard with the gloved fingers of his left hand. "Moderation is for monks," he muttered, quoting the wisdom of Lazarus Long.

A chill went down his sweaty back. The cold air was creeping in.

I wonder how far they went before setting up camp,? he pondered, as his eyes focused on the thin ski tracks in front of him. He slung '"Old Gerry"' back on, tightened the hip belt, cinched his pole straps, and pushed off with a kick.

Eager to forget about his aches and pains, he let his mind drift back to the summer of 1963.

CHAPTER 2

—◦❈◦—

"The first thing ya gotta do is get bait."
Uncle Art was standing over him, leaning on his crutches. He had a big smile and a twinkle in his soft blue eyes as he looked down at the eight-year-old boy. The kid sat slumped over, on the edge of one of the many feather-beds in the old log cabin, wishing he could crawl under the patchwork quilt he was sitting on and disappear.

Why doesn't he have any of his own kids to bully? the boy was thinking, drenched in self -pity. In response to his own question, his thoughts turned mean. *I s"pose it's ''cause he's a cripple.*

The cruel thought jolted Bob back to the present. He recalled that he didn't find out until he grew up that Uncle Art's kind, wonderful wife Mary was the one who was unable to have children. A real shame, since they both adored kids. That's the type of people who should have them.

It occurred to Bob that he and his Luce Line trail companions didn't have children. For his friends it was by chance. For him, it was by choice.

He frowned and shook his head in disgust. *What a selfish little shit I was,* he snorted at the memory. *But I was just a kid.*

He tried to think about something else, but the recollection drew him back in with even more clarity.

"What kinda bait? Do ya know, Bobby?" his great uncle asked excitedly.

He *hated* being called Bobby. Kids in the neighborhood called him "Bobby Sox," because, when he was five, his mother had made him wear knee-high socks to school. She thought they were cute. On the playground, one of his sister's friends – "Evil Linda" – said that it looked like he had on bobby socks. Lots of kids were there. The name stuck until he started junior high. It made life at school miserable. He decided that, when he grew up, the first thing that he was going to do was change his name to Bart or Duke or something like that. Anything but Bobby.

On this cold January night, Bob – not Bart or Duke – was amused at the irony that he was wearing knee-high socks right now – in fact he'd been wearing them with his skiing knickers for the past twenty-five years.

He – and his friends – could never get into the idea of wearing one-piece ski suits. They believed that "real" men should not wear Spandex. Period. End of discussion. Of course that was a rule they would all later violate. As usual, John would be the instigator. He was the educated one – "Mister High-Tech". He even had a computer at home.

By the time Bob had started cross-country skiing at age fifteen, the "Bobby Socks" trauma had been overshadowed by subsequent traumas and would get buried even deeper as he got older.

As for "Evil Linda," she was patiently waiting for Bob to come home from yet another adventure with his friends. They had gotten married in 1984. A terrible event the year before had brought them together, but he didn't want to think about that. He consciously blocked out the memory and went back to his youth.

An image of Linda's laughing face at nine years old came to focus in his mind. *Maybe she fell in love with me on the playground, wearing my bobby sox*, he laughed to himself.

He was stunned by how clear his memories were tonight. Most of them he hadn't recalled in decades. It was as if the vast heavens above him had opened up a portal to his soul and the contents were spilling out. He had skied on clear, cold nights like this before – dozens of times – but it never had this kind of effect on him.

"There's something strange about this prairie," he muttered, bewildered. "And this sky. It's like they're trying to communicate with me."

The word "Cosmos" popped into his head.

"Yeah, that's it," he let out a sigh of relief. "The name of that town is helping my mind play tricks on me." He frowned and looked up at the stars as a sadness fell over him.

No one had called him "Bobby Sox" in a very long time. His wife never did and everyone else who had was either dead or had descended into the dark reaches of his past. The hated nickname would probably receive a warm welcome if it could bring back any of those people.

His pace slowed to a crawl as his mind slipped back in time.

—◦⊗◦—

"The bait you need depends on what you're fishin' for."

Uncle Art's gravelly voice was getting excited.

"Today we're gonna fish for punkinseeds. Do ya know what punkinseeds bite on?"

Feeling beat up and badgered, Bobby slowly shook his head "no".

"Why, they like angleworms."

Oh great, thought Bobby. He hated angleworms. They were slimy and disgusting.

A bully up the street from their house made him put one in his mouth once. Just the thought made him sick to his stomach.

"We need to get some before we go fishin'," Uncle Art said, matter-of-factly. "Do ya know the best place to get angleworms?"

The store, thought Bobby. He was a city kid. Everything came from the store. *Wait a minute!* Bobby thought excitedly, *its' Sunday isn't it? Yeah, sure it is! He saw Uncle Art and Aunt Mary get into their big Cadillac this morning! They were all dressed up and going to church! Stores are closed on Sundays! If the store is closed, we can't get bait, and if we can't get bait, we can't go fishing!*

Bobby looked up at Uncle Art with a big smile.

Uncle Art caught the smile and beamed it back at him.

"Under the cabin!" he said, almost laughing.

Bobby's eyes got big and his mouth dropped wide open. His glee turned to horror.

There's a troll under the cabin! His mind raced in fear. *Everybody knows it! My sister and my cousins have been telling me about it since I was four. I think I even saw it once!*

Great Grandpa Martin had built the cabin right on top of a spring-fed brook that flowed into the lake. There was a trap door in the wooden floor of the kitchen where the women used to drop a bucket on a rope down into the brook to get water for cooking. They didn't do it anymore, because, according to the adults, the water went bad when a house was built upstream.

But all the kids knew the truth. They stopped getting water because the troll lived down there.

Bobby stammered, "We-we-we can't go under the cabin!" His eyes were as big as silver dollars.

"Well *I* can't," Uncle Art said sadly. "Not anymore." He seemed reflective as he looked out toward the lake.

"Your grandpa used to have me get 'em under there when we were younger," his large torso was slumping deeper into his crutches, "but I don't fit anymore." Uncle Art paused for so long that Bobby thought he had forgotten about going fishing. To a little boy, a minute can seem like forever. Then Uncle Art perked up, "But you can fit! I'll show you the best spot to find "em."

Bobby sat frozen on the bed and squeezed his eyes shut real hard, thinking, *Maybe this will all just go away if I wish hard enough.*

Bob's senses snapped back to his current reality.

"Never got that one to work," he chuckled. "It would've come in handy a few times."

The sky was getting deeper and darker, and the stars seemed to explode across the black canvas. Real winter night was settling in.

"Where the hell are those guys?"

He was ready to stop and relax with some hot food, lively arguing, a couple of drinks, and a warm sleeping bag. His kick was beginning to slip, and the glide was getting worse. The snirt was like sandpaper, peeling the wax off of his skis.

Didn't figure I'd have to do this again tonight. He stopped, took off '"Old Gerry"' and unzipped one of the pouches. The stuff sack that held ski wax fell into his hand.

His thoughts drifted back to Lake Hanging Horn.

Bobby got up off the bed. His body was stiff and his legs felt like boat anchors as he followed Uncle Art to the screen door, his great uncle's crutches clumping heavily on the shiny wooden floor of the old log cabin.

Oh great, Bobby thought, *that noise is going to wake up the troll.*

It was a beautiful late-summer day. The sun was shining, with not a cloud in the sky.

Bobby looked around. His dad and grandpa were playing horseshoes with the people who had the cabin next to them. He could hear the high-pitched laughter and voices of the women as they were starting to put together supper in the big kitchen in the cabin (even though it had been only an hour or so since lunch). The smell of smoke from the two gigantic wood stoves filled the air. Birds were chirping in the dense, green canopy above him. His sister and cousins were splashing happily along the lake-shore, catching frogs and chasing minnows.

Bobby's youth kept him from realizing that life just didn't get any better than that. All he could think about was how he was going to be eaten by the troll.

Will he chew on me first? Or swallow me in one big gulp? When I'm gone, they'll be so sorry for making me do this. His head hung so low that it almost fell off. *But wait! Bobby thought, Uncle Art said that he's been under the cabin!* Bobby's head lifted up, and his heart followed, but they both quickly sank again. *That was when he was young. Uncle Art is so old, that it was probably before the troll was even born.*

Bobby trudged to the edge of the cabin, right out-side the kitchen. The loud, laughing, soprano voices of the women blasted out through an open window.

"They won't even hear me scream," he mumbled to himself, lips trembling, engulfed in self-pity.

"Down there." Uncle Art pointed at the darkness under the cabin.

The brook was a channel carved through the rich soil of the forest floor. It was about two feet wide at the bottom, ten feet wide at the top, and at least eight feet from the trap door in the kitchen floor to the surface of the water. It meandered diagonally under the cabin. To Bobby, it might as well have been the entrance to hell.

He looked up at Uncle Art as a dog would in fear of being punished for crapping on the carpet. His great uncle didn't seem to pick up on the look of terror on Bobby's young face.

"See there, by the coffee grinds?" Art's hand was pointing like the finger of God in the Sistine Chapel.

Hands down, the beverage of choice at the old cabin was coffee. It was brewing all the time. At least two blue enamel pots were on the wood stoves at any moment, and, frequently, a ten-quart aluminum percolator was simmering in the big gathering room where everyone sat to play cards, checkers, or cribbage, or to put together a puzzle on the cool, damp evenings and rainy days. The cabin never had a TV. A large RCA Victor radio stood in a corner of the main room, but Bobby had never heard it turned on. He figured it was at least a hundred years old and didn't work.

All that coffee, for all those years, created a mountain of coffee grounds, and all of it had been dumped around the cabin. Most of it right outside the kitchen door. Right where Uncle Art was pointing.

Gee, maybe that's what made the brook water rancid, thought Bob. The revelation made him stop skiing for a moment to ponder the thought. He never saw any garbage hauled away from the lake place. All the organic stuff went into the woods or under the cabin. The rest was burned in a fifty-five gallon drum by the road – about a hundred feet behind the old log structure, – in a little clearing full of thistles, next to the brook. Bob shrugged his shoulders and let his mind go back to that warm summer day.

Bobby got on his hands and knees and crawled into the darkness.

I wonder if my sister will cry at my funeral,? he was thinking as his hands sunk into the soft, moist earth that was mostly made up of decayed coffee grounds.

"That's it!" Uncle Art said, obviously excited. "Get some of that good dirt, too."

He handed Bobby a shiny Folgers coffee can that he seemed to have produced out of nowhere.

"Just dig into that dirt – you'll see"

Bobby's trembling hand pawed the ground. Something wet and slimy appeared just as his eyes were starting to get used to the dim light. Yes, it was an angleworm. A big one.

"Yuch!" he said out loud, shaking it off his hand into the coffee can.

"Ohh! That's a good one!" Uncle Art's encouraging voice wasn't helping. "Go down a little deeper, that's it!"

Bobby crawled farther into the darkness. He dug up several more worms and put them into the can. *I guess this isn't so bad,* he thought, *pretty disgusting, but I guess I'll live through it.* He was starting to get used to lying down there.

"But wait! What about the troll?!" Bobby muttered, nervously digging out two more worms.

"How many do we need?" Bobby's squeaky voice called out of the darkness.

"How many ya got?" Uncle Art responded.

"Six."

"Oh, a couple more'll do."

Bobby reached ahead. His hand touched something furry.

He heard a growl, then two angry, yellow eyes opened and stared back at him, about four inches from his face

"THE TROLL!" he shrieked, and he started to back up fast, his blue jeans slipping on the damp dirt. His back banged against the support logs under the cabin, and he dropped the coffee can, which rolled down the embankment and splashed into the brook. The dark form brushed past him, snarling and hissing. It bolted from the shadows and loped off into the underbrush, as Bobby got a glimpse of its' tail.

"It's a raccoon!" he yelled, gasping for breath so that very little sound came out. Bobby's heart was pounding so hard, he was sure that the women in the kitchen above him could hear it. But they just kept on laughing and talking. He had almost died of fright, and they didn't even notice. Typical moms.

"Ohh! That was a big one, wasn't it? "Uncle Art was laughing. "You sure scared him!"

Bobby was lying in the coffee grounds, face down, half under the cabin. He had thought he was going to die, but he didn't. He took a minute to collect his senses.

"Scared him?" he whispered, "You've got to be kidding!" Then a wry smile formed on his young lips. *Could that be the troll all the kids are afraid of?*

Bobby's face was covered with dirt and coffee grounds. His heart-beat was gradually slowing down. It might not explode out of his chest after all.

"I dropped the can," he yelled to Uncle Art.

"Oh. Well, can you get it?' Uncle Art yelled back.

"Yeah," Bobby said, as he was backing out from under the cabin.

He got on his hands and knees and started to wipe the loose dirt off his white t – shirt and sweaty face. He was numb, but he wasn't afraid any more.

"Did ya get the can?" Uncle Art asked eagerly.

"No. But I will."

Bobby got up and walked over to a stump and sat down. He pulled up his blue jeans and took off his sneakers and then his socks.

"Whatcha gonna do?" Art implored, confused.

"Get the can," Bobby replied.

He walked to a spot about twenty feet from the back of the cabin where the embankment wasn't so steep, slid down it, and stood in the brook.

Uncle Art had followed him part of the way. He was leaning on his crutches with a puzzled look on his face. He hadn't heard the can splash into the water.

Bobby walked down the brook, following it under the old log building. The can had landed open side up in about four inches of water. Luckily, this time of year, the water level was usually low. He picked up the coffee can and checked the contents. All the worms he had caught were still inside.

He surveyed his surroundings. He saw the brook flowing out from under the cabin to the lake. It was at least a hundred feet away. He looked up and saw the old White Pine logs – now gray with age – that held up the cabin, and he saw the trap door that led up to the kitchen.

"I'll bet nobody has seen the trap door from the bottom before," he said to himself.

His chest welled up with pride. He felt powerful, invincible.

"How ya doin' down there?"

"Fine. I'll be right out." He started walking down the brook to the back of the cabin. Then he remembered that he needed to get two more angleworms. Without fear, he crawled up the steep bank. As he got to the top, he looked up.

Scratched into the wooden frame around the trap door were the initials "AC."

He leaned back, confused. Someone else had been here before him! *But who? "AC"?" Who could that be?*

"How ya doin', son?" Uncle Art's raspy voice was low and soft.

It hit Bobby like a brick. *"AC"?" Does that mean Art Christianson?*

"Oh my gosh," Bobby muttered to himself, his eyes welling up with tears, " He's been here to." "Here I was, so afraid, and he's been here too, as a little crippled boy."

Uncle Art had said that he got angleworms from under the cabin, but you could find them right along the edges. How did he get to the trap door without the use of his legs? If Uncle Art's brother (Bobby's grandpa) had helped him, wouldn't his initials be there too?

Bobby fought back the tears. He felt embarrassed and ashamed.

"Just give me a minute," his quavering voice yelled back to his great uncle.

He reached into his back pocket and pulled out the pearl-handled pocket-knife that his dad gave him for his birthday, just a few weeks before.

Bobby climbed up to the top of the embankment and snapped open the blade.

It was a long reach for his eight-year-old arms, but the tip of the blade made contact with the old rough-hewn pine.

He carved "BS" right next to "AC".

"Bobby Sorenson was here too," he said. His stoic words were low and soft.

On his way out from under the cabin, he grabbed a handful of dirt. There were at least two more angle-worms in it. He dropped the dirt with the worms into the can. That would do it.

He stood up along the edge of the cabin. Uncle Art was looking at him intently. But the laughter that made his uncle's eyes twinkle had been replaced with something else. Bobby had seen that look before, in his dad's eyes. It was the look his dad had given him when he learned how to ride a bicycle.

"Did you find what you were looking for?" Uncle Art's voice was slow and deep.

Bobby looked into his uncle's big, warm eyes and nodded solemnly.

Uncle Art looked down at the coffee can that Bobby was holding. He could see the pocket-knife in Bobby's hand, up against the can.

A broad smile slowly spread across his face and the twinkle returned to his eyes.

"Ya know, that troll was there when I was a kid, too," he said softly.

Bobby looked up at him and smiled.

"Let's go fishin', Uncle Art."

CHAPTER 3

The lights of Prinsburg were just ahead.

Bob had finished re-waxing his skis and pushed on. Just on the edge of town, he saw a grotesque figure about twenty feet from the old railroad grade. He squinted to get a better look. It was a turkey – the white, domestic variety – frozen, eyes open, in a running position. It apparently had escaped a nearby farm during the storm. This was as far as it had gotten. *How bizarre,* he thought, *frozen dead in its tracks.* It gave him yet another insight into how really terrible the storm had been. Snowstorms were bad in the city, but nothing like they get out here. If he hadn't seen the turkey with his own eyes, he wouldn't have believed it.

He glided into town. *It must be about 10:30 and another town is boarded up for the night.* The soft, stifled glow of a few streetlights was the only indication that there might be civilization here. All Midwesterners know that January is a mean month, especially in the open spaces, and better off left alone.

The nights are particularly brutal. You only venture out into it when you have to.

"Or if you're stupid skiers," Bob snorted out loud. He skated out of town, his newly awakened mind allowing another memory from his distant past to wander into his thoughts.

He had only gone fishing once before his experience with Uncle Art.

It had been in the spring of the same year – the "Season Opener."

His dad and one of his dad's buddies from work had taken him and that man's son up north to Lake Trelipee. It was a beautiful lake, nestled between high hills covered with birch, maple, and pine trees. The family camped there during the summer.

Bobby was all excited when his dad had asked him if he wanted to come along, because it meant that he was growing up. He felt important as he helped his dad pack their "56 Ford convertible with fishing poles, a minnow bucket, army surplus sleeping bags, a tackle box, and two duffel bags full of "fishing" clothes. It was his first big adventure – his rite of passage into manhood. Or so he thought. There would be many, many more to follow.

His mom fussed over him like she was guarding her chick until he pushed her away with embarrassed indignation. She told him to turn his collar up, keep his feet dry, and dress warm. "You can always take some of the clothes off," she said. He had never been fussed over like that before – not even when he had the chicken pox.

(*Nor have I since then,* Bob thought, a slight pang of nostalgia creeping in.)

Bobby's sister stood half in-half out of the front door as they drove off, looking at him with tears of envy. She had never been asked to go fishing, and she was going to be twelve soon. She loved her little brother, but that day, hate wasn't very far away.

"It was a different time," Bob sighed at the recollection, "Such a very different time." As his skis carried him into the future, his thoughts remained in the past.

Bobby and his dad drove over to his buddy's house. They transferred all of their gear into his station wagon as Bobby protested. He wanted to take his dad's convertible. He loved that car.

He loved riding in it with the top down as they cruised around Lake Nokomis and went to the Dairy Queen on hot summer evenings with his sister and their friends.

On those days, his dad was the king of the neighborhood, and Bobby was the prince.

But his dad's buddy's car had a trailer hitch, and they needed that to pull the boat, his dad explained "and there's not enough room for us and all of our gear in our convertible."

The drive was incredibly long. Bobby thought the car smelled funny, like moldy socks or something worse, and the other boy was very quiet. He was a couple of years older than Bobby, and he had been on fishing trips before. Occasionally, he would dart fierce glances over at Bobby. When he wasn't glaring, his eyes had a look of dread in them.

Bobby missed his sister. She always found a way to make long car rides go by faster.

They got to the rented cabin after midnight. It sat between big pine trees, right on the shore of the lake. His dad said it was a pretty setting, but it was too dark for them to see it. The air was damp and cold, and the stars were masked by clouds. Bobby saw white patches on the ground, in the woods, and by the cabin. This was very confusing. *Snow? That can't be. It was warm and sunny today,* he thought. He hadn't seen any snow by his house in the city in over a month.

The cabin was filthy. And there were mice. Lots of mice.

His dad tried to get an old pot-belly wood-burning stove to light, but the fire kept going out, and it got smoky in the cabin. They had to open the windows to let the smoke out, and that made it even colder inside. Bobby could see his breath. His dad said there must be something blocking the flue (whatever that was) – maybe a squirrel nest or something. He decided that they would check it out in the morning, but first they should just hit the sack and get some sleep.

So far the trip wasn't what Bobby expected.

Bobby shivered inside his thin sleeping bag and listened to the mice having a party in the walls and ceiling all around them. He knew that he slept with his mouth open – his sister had told him this many times – and she had even complained to their Mom about it. Their mom just laughed, saying that their dad slept with his mouth open too. Bobby just prayed that no mouse would crawl into his mouth while he was sleeping. He wished he was back at home, in his warm bed, with the covers tucked tightly around him. He fell asleep to the loud snoring of his dad's buddy. Maybe a mouse would crawl into *his* mouth instead.

Bob smiled at the recollection. He scrubbed some ice off his beard with his fingers.

His legs were getting stiff. "Old Gerry" was bearing down heavily on his shoulders.

It's at least ten degrees colder than when I started, he thought, *maybe I should just find some kind of shelter and catch up with the guys tomorrow."*

His stubbornness made him push on – that and the knowledge that Doug and John would have no problem with the idea of taking off without him in the morning.

He had spent years letting them get way ahead of him while skiing or biking only to catch up with them and leave them in the dust after they thought they had finally ditched him. They didn't find this endearing. That might be why they skied so far the first day. They knew Bob could take care of himself, and if he picked up a little humility by having to work harder to catch them, that would be okay too. Bob set his jaw. *No, I'll catch up with them tonight. No matter what.*

He put his aches and pains out of his mind by focusing on the past.

—◦❁◦—

Bobby awoke to the sound of a large wooden spoon banging on a cast iron skillet.

It was still dark outside. The noisemaker was his dad.

"Rise and shine! Daylight in the swamp!"

He had heard his dad say this many times. He always thought it was funny.

But not today. Those other times were car camping trips. He'd hear his mom and sister groan as they slowly woke up in the big canvas umbrella tent. He and his dad would laugh, and when their eyes met, a bond formed between them.

But, today, he looked at his father's laughing eyes with contempt.

His dad saw his look and laughed louder. "C'mon! It's time to go fishin'! We gotta get on the lake before the fish wake up!"

"Let the fish sleep!" Bobby yelled back, rolling over to look away from his dad.

His dad laughed even harder. "C'mon, son! Don't be a spoil sport."

Bobby looked down. There was a patch of ice on his sleeping bag where he had been breathing. His mouth tasted like it was full of mouse turds. He did not want to get up, even though he was very hungry. It had been a long time since he had eaten the cheese and baloney sandwich his mom had made for him. That was last night. In the car right after they left his dad's buddy's house. It seemed like a long time ago.

"Gotta get some grub in your belly before we go out on the lake!" his dad beamed.

Mysteriously, he had gotten the wood stove to work, and on it was a big kettle of oatmeal. Bobby didn't like oatmeal. It was okay if it had brown sugar on it, but he'd rather have his mom's pancakes, with maple syrup. Or a bowl of frosted flakes.

He sat up on his cot. It was getting warmer in the cabin. A frozen spitcicle slid off his sleeping bag and shattered on the floor. His dad handed him a plastic bowl with oatmeal in it. It was warm, not hot.

"Where's the brown sugar?" Bobby asked.

"We don't have any," his dad replied sternly. "Just eat."

The other two were just beginning to stir. The other boy looked at Bobby with tired eyes.

How come his dad isn't grumpy at him, Bobby wondered, spooning a thick clump of oatmeal into his mouth. It was awful. Tasted like mouse turds.

They put their gear into the boat as it started to get light out. There were a few other boats on the water already. The sky was slate gray – and even darker at the far end of the lake. A slight breeze was coming from across the water.

Waves were lapping at the sides of the boat as they headed out across the water to his dad's "secret spot." The outboard motor sounded erratic as it bounced over the waves, which got bigger in the middle of the lake. Bobby's dad motioned to his buddy to slow the motor down.

"Get yer poles out," his dad said to the boys.

"I can't," Bobby replied. "My hands are frozen."

"Aw, buck up." His dad's piercing eyes told him that it would be a good idea to pick up his fishing pole. "And get a minnow out of the bucket." His dad's tone of voice meant business.

They had stopped at a bait shop in Princeton the night before. Bobby thought there must've been about a thousand cars there. Even though it took his dad almost an hour to get the minnows, the boys weren't allowed out of the car. In the parking lot, there were a lot of other boys, in a lot of other cars. None of them could get out either. They were like sad, captive monkeys, and they all had the same look of dread on their faces.

Bobby was beginning to understand why. When his dad and his dad's buddy got back in the car, they argued all the way to the cabin. His dad was mad because he thought that his buddy had said that he was going to get bait before they left the city. His buddy was mad for the same reason, but in reverse. Bobby would not have been surprised to find out that they were both wrong. The men had never discussed it when planning the trip.

Bobby reached into the minnow bucket. The water was like ice cubes. He got a slippery, squirming minnow out. It flipped out of his frozen hands and went over the side of the boat. The sound of it hitting the water was almost inaudible. Just, "blip."

His dad's buddy somehow heard the sound. He turned and yelled at Bobby. "Hey, kid! Whatta ya doin'? Feedin' the fish?"

The other boy slid across the seat away from Bobby. He seemed afraid that he would get yelled at too, just for sitting next to him.

Bobby's dad leaned forward and said softly, "Get another one, son."

Bobby reached into the bucket and got another minnow.

His dad helped him rig it up. He called the tackle a "spinner." It was disgusting. He showed Bobby how to shove a wire down the throat of the minnow until it came out it's butt, then you put a big triple hook on the end.

I'll bet that doesn't feel good, thought Bobby. He wondered what it would feel like to have a wire shoved in his mouth and out his butt. The vision of this made his stomach turn. He could taste the oatmeal coming back up. *At least we're not using angleworms! I hate angleworms!* The thought of those slimy things didn't make his stomach feel any better.

"Nice Walleye chop," his dad's buddy said, breaking the silence.

Bobby had no idea what that meant. *So...they were going to chop wall eyes? How do you do that?* He was afraid to ask. Nobody explained.

The motor puttered along erratically. A long silence passed.

His dad's buddy said, "Let's pull up anchor- and move to another part of the lake." Bobby knew what an anchor looked like, but he had never seen them put one in the water. They didn't even have one with them. So how could you pull one up?

His dad said they should just keep "trolling."

"Trolling!? Really? Is that what we're doing?" Bobby thought back to previous summers at Lake Hanging Horn. His mind started racing in panic. *Are we trying to catch the troll at Great Grandpa's cabin? Or is this a different troll? Why is the troll in the water? Do all lakes have trolls? Would they really be able to catch it with fishing rods and minnows!?* For a little boy on his first fishing trip, it was very confusing – but nobody offered an explanation.

Meanwhile, as they sat on the lake, Bobby's dad and his buddy argued most of the time- or else they told stories about huge fish they had caught. (Bobby was very suspicious of these stories. He had never seen his dad bring home a big fish from one of his trips, and his dad went on a lot of fishing trips.)

They argued about car body styles and "horse-power" and just about anything else a person could think of. The only thing they seemed to agree on was that they each had a "huge mortgage" and a "ball and chain" that was holding them down. Bobby wanted to ask them what these things were so that he could avoid them when he got older, but, being a boy, he figured he would find out soon enough. It seemed to be a man thing. And now that he knew what their names were, he would be on the lookout for them. The motor puttered on, occasionally coughing and lurching. It wasn't getting any warmer. Or brighter. Around noon, a fine mist swept across the lake. It quickly turned to drizzle. The misery continued.

"Well, it's time for a little lunch," his dad blurted out, though none of them could really tell what time it was since there was no sun.

The morning's light breeze had grown stronger as the day wore on. Between that and the rain, it chilled Bobby right to the bone. As everyone slowly got soaked, the conversation between the two men had dwindled.

His dad got out the brown paper bag that held lunch for the boys. More cheese and baloney sandwiches, wrapped in wax paper – which were now soggy. His mom had put in a small bag of Fritos, but the older boy snatched that away from Bobby and hid it in his rain poncho before Bobby could get to it. A fierce stare told Bobby that he had better not say anything.

The other boy's dad said, "We should have a contest to see who catches the first fish."

Bobby's dad argued that it should be for the biggest fish.

Bobby looked vacantly at his father. In his misery, he had forgotten that what they were doing was fishing.

I thought we were trolling, he pondered. No matter. He shrugged his shoulders and continued to eat his soggy sandwich. It tasted like school paste.

His hands were frozen, limply hanging on to his Zebco fishing rod.

He thought, *My minnow should be getting a nice swim. That is, if it doesn't mind having a wire down its throat, coming out its' butt.*

He longed for the mouse – ridden cabin. And warm oatmeal without brown sugar.

He tried to remember "home" but his brain was numb. He thought he had a sister, but he couldn't remember what she looked like. *If she saw what fishing was like, she wouldn't feel so bad that she didn't get to go.*

The time dragged on. At one point Bobby looked up, water running down his nose, and gazed across the lake. All the other boats were gone. They were the smart ones. He looked down and fell back into a stupor. More time dragged on.

Then, all of a sudden, Bobby's fishing rod lurched out of his hands.

His dad grabbed it before it went overboard.

"Cut the motor! Cut the motor!" his dad yelled.

The low drone sputtered out. The only sound they heard was the high-pitched whine as fishing line was being torn from Bobby's Zebco reel – at lightning speed. His dad put the rod back into Bobby's hands and firmly cupped his own hands over Bobby's.

Bobby's heart was racing. *Have I caught the troll?* he thought. *What am I supposed to do?* His eyes searched his father's, looking for answers.

His dad read his thoughts. "Just hold on tight, son."

The whining sound slowed down, then quit altogether. The fishing line went limp.

"Reel it in slowly, son"

The other man started pulling the rope to start the motor.

"No – don't!" Bobby's dad yelled. "Just give it a minute."

The other man swore under his breath. He obviously was not pleased that Bobby had been the first one to catch something.

Bobby heard a crunching sound. The other boy figured it was a good time to eat those Fritos – no one would notice with all this commotion. Another glare told Bobby that he'd better keep his mouth shut. Bobby reeled his fishing line in slowly, his dad's hands still over his. They were warm. *How could they be warm when his dad had held a fishing pole for as long as he had?*

The boat was drifting in the direction of the fishing line. Right back to his dad's "secret spot."

They had been criss–crossing it all day. It had been another source of argument between his dad and his buddy, but it looked like it finally paid off.

Bobby hadn't noticed until now, but the lake had gotten calm, and the drizzle had turned to fog. He kept slowly reeling in the fishing line. Once his dad noticed tension on it, he told Bobby to stop.

They drifted quietly for about five minutes. For a little boy with frozen hands, it seemed like an eternity. An eternity within another eternity. The only sound was the soft crunching of Fritos being eaten by the other boy sitting beside him. Bobby gave the boy a look of disgust. Then, responding to his father's direction, Bobby started reeling in again. The fishing line began hitting the water at a steeper angle.

"Get the net," his dad said to the other boy in a loud whisper.

The startled boy jumped up, dropping the bag of Fritos. The men were so focused on the fishing line, they didn't notice.

"Quiet now!" Bobby's dad yelled, a little louder than a whisper.

The boy banged the net on the side of the aluminum boat. It sounded like a gunshot across the lake. Bobby was sure he hadn't meant to do it. He was just nervous.

Everything seemed to go into slow motion.

His dad reached for the net, letting go of Bobby's hands.

Bobby squinted to get a better look at the water where his line penetrated the surface. Something was emerging.

It looked like a small submarine. It was half as long as the boat.

"That's no troll," Bobby muttered under his breath.

The big fish rolled it's large, flat eyes. It was looking right at him.

"Muskie!" his Dad yelled out as he swung the net over the side of the boat.

This seemed absurd. There was no way that fish was going to fit in the net. Even Bobby could see that. Its' head couldn't fit in the net.

The fish rolled onto its' back as his dad took a swipe at it. The net brushed the tail of the fish, and it disappeared below the surface and was gone like a shot.

Bobby's reel started whining again, returning the boat to real time.

"Don't touch the line!" his dad yelled, but it was too late, as Bobby's left hand closed tightly over the rod just above the reel, supporting his right hand, which was gripping the plastic handle as hard as it could..

It was only about twenty seconds before the whining of the line stopped suddenly when they heard the "ping" as the last of the line left the reel.

Everyone sat in silence for a long minute. The calm was deafening until his dad's buddy yelled angrily, "You shoulda had that one! If I got the motor goin', it'd be in the boat right now!"

His dad yelled back, "Like hell!" and the two men started to argue again.

The other boy leaned forward to Bobby and said, "I'm sorry."

Bobby responded, "That's okay. Did you see the size of that thing? There's no way we could have gotten that fish into the boat. And if we did, it would've eaten us."

"No. I mean about the Fritos."

Bobby smiled.

The older boy smiled back, then reached down and picked up the bag of corn chips. It had landed open – end up in the two inches of water in the bottom of the boat. There was about half a bag left. He offered some to Bobby, then got a puzzled look on his face.

"What's wrong with your hand?" he asked.

Bobby looked over and noticed that his left hand – still tightly clenching the rod, where it had been since the big fish took off – was dripping red into the water at their feet. He opened it slowly, cocking his head curiously at what he saw. He had never seen so much blood.

Then his hand started to sting.

"Dad! Look!" he blurted out.

"Oh shit!" his dad shouted, turning away from his buddy to look at Bobby's hand. "I told you not to touch the line!"

Bobby started sobbing softly – not because his hand hurt, but because his dad was mad at him – and had sworn at him, too!

"It's okay," his dad said more softly. "It's okay. It's just a line cut. It'll heal. It'll just be a little sore for a while." His dad pulled a damp handkerchief out of his back pocket, and wrapped it around Bobby's hand. Bobby watched as the handkerchief soon turned pink.

As this was happening, Bobby realized that his dad's buddy had been trying to start the motor. It popped once, then quit. He pulled, and pulled – and pulled on the cord – but to no avail. Bobby's dad told him to check the gas.

"It's not the gas!" he yelled back. "This motor will run all day on a tank of gas!"

It's been all day, Bobby thought, since it looked like it was getting darker out.

The man pulled the motor rope a few more times, then crossed his arms and sat with an angry look on his face. "Christ," he said under his breath, as he checked the small gas tank on the old, beat up motor. He didn't want to be proven wrong, especially not by Bobby's dad. Where they worked, he was Bobby's dad's boss. He'd never live it down.

"Gimme the gas can!" he yelled at his son.

The boy looked around, turned to him, and shrugged his shoulders. No gas can was to be found in the small boat.

"Don't tell me you forgot the damn gas can!" the boy's father yelled, a wild look showing in his eyes. His son cowered and drew away from him.

"It's the responsibility of the one running the motor to remember the gas," Bobby's dad said with authority, looking squarely at the other man. The other boy's dad jerked his eyes away from his son to glare at his subordinate. They stared at each other for a few seconds, but the other man couldn't hold the stare.

"Well, goddammit, then I guess we'll have to paddle," he swore, looking away.

Bobby felt sorry for the other boy. He glanced over at him. The kid was smirking under the hood of his rain poncho. He was getting pleasure out of seeing his dad being reprimanded for a change. *As luck would have it, the boat had no oars.* They all used their hands to paddle across the lake. Not another word was spoken during the many hours it took to reach the far shore, now well after dark.

Bobby was so grateful to be back on land, he felt like kissing the ground. His left hand was throbbing and his right hand was frozen from paddling. "God, I hate fishing," he said to himself as he dragged his feet across the yard to the cold cabin. Dread washed over him like a wet blanket, and he moaned out loud as a horrible thought leaked into his throbbing soggy brain: *And we have to do this tomorrow, too.*

CHAPTER 4

"**B**ut fishing with Uncle Art was different," Bob said, under his breath.

He stopped skiing. He had been so immersed in the memory of that day on the lake, that he momentarily forgot where he was. The sky crashed in on him. He felt dizzy, nauseated. He lost his balance and almost fell down.

I'm getting dehydrated. He took off his pack and got out his Scotch and water, wishing it was just water. Or Gatorade.

"Where are those guys?" he asked himself. "Did I pass them while I was daydreaming?"

Panic flashed through him for a split second. It was an old, uncomfortable feeling, dating back to when he was seven, and had been ditched by his sister and her friends on a bus trip into downtown Minneapolis. He had only been alone for a few minutes, but he never forgot the feeling. They thought it was funny, but when they saw how scared he was, they made him swear that he wouldn't tell his mom and dad.

He never did tell them. His sister was so grateful, that she told him, "I'm sorry," about a hundred times.

He knew it hadn't been her idea, though, and a new level of trust developed between them, beginning with that incident.

Bob thought he had grown out of that fear of being left behind long ago, but even as an adult, you never really do. You just steer away from the things that will get you there.

He looked down the trail. A wave of relief, then embarrassment, passed over him.

A fresh set of ski tracks led away from him, heading east.

"Well duh," he snickered. "It's not like I'm alone in the Yukon or something."

A justification for his brief fear conveniently popped into his head.

It's all those stars. They're intimidating me. It's mind-boggling.

He took his pole straps off and shook his hands. They had gone numb. The palm of his left hand was stinging – that still happened when that hand got cold.

The damp handkerchief that Bobby's dad had wrapped his hand in while on the boat on that cold April day so long ago, had been dirty. The Mercurochrome bottle in the rented cabin was empty. Neither of the men had brought any first aid supplies with them on the fishing trip. Back in those days, it never crossed their minds. That was the kind of thing "the women" would pack, and "the women" were not on that trip.

After they got home, the fishing-line cut got infected, and a red line appeared on the inside of Bobby's left forearm, so his mom took him to the doctor. They gave him a shot and some pills and wrapped up his hand with gauze and funny-smelling cream. He had to keep it bandaged for a couple of months that spring, going into summer. His dad felt so bad about it, that he gave Bobby a beautiful pearl-handled pocket knife for his birthday – instead of the new fishing pole he had already bought for his son. Bobby never saw the fishing pole. He didn't even know that his dad had bought it until his sister told him about it years later.

Bob ignored the sting in his palm, slipped his gloves back on, cinched his pack, and shuffled forward, his skis finding the track that his friends had set. His weary mind wandered back in time.

Yes, fishing with Uncle Art was definitely different. Bob smiled as he returned to the memory.

For one thing, it was done in summer.

It was a warm, lazy day – the kind of day that Midwesterners dream about all winter, then usually bitch about it when it finally comes. "It's too humid." "It's too windy." "It's too dusty." "There are too many bugs." Or just plain "It's too hot." They can't help it. It's in their nature to complain.

Maybe it's because of their predominantly German and Scandinavian heritage. Or maybe it's the harsh extremes of the climate they live in. The rugged people that Bob had spent his whole life with were usually not even aware they were complaining; they just did. It was second nature to them.

Bob had worked outside his entire adult life – first as a land surveyor, then as a construction manager, and now as a building contractor. He knew there were only twenty-two "perfect" weather days in a year in this part of the country. No more, no less. These were the days where it *wasn't* too hot, too cold, too windy, too buggy, or too anything else. They were usually split up pretty evenly. Half at the end of April, half in the beginning of September.

The day he went fishing with Uncle Art, Bob would've picked as one of those twenty-two days – a rare August gem.

Uncle Art and Bobby headed out across Lake Hanging Horn in a homemade wide-bottom fishing boat. The boat was a masterfully crafted, beautifully constructed vessel built thirty years before Bobby was born. It was built by a bachelor Norwegian nephew of Great Grandpa Martin.

The boat glided through the water like it was proud to be there. It had been meticulously painted dark forest green on the outer shell and glossy white on the inside. Everybody on the lake knew that boat. It had never been anywhere else. The young carpenter had built it right on the shore in front of the log cabin, using wood that had been cut off the property. It was rumored that it took him three seasons to build. It was worth it.

Uncle Art's three-horsepower Johnson outboard motor pushed the boat across the water with ease. Bobby didn't know how amazing that was. The wooden boat weighed at least six hundred pounds – empty. It was over twenty feet long ("forty hands"

Great Grandpa Martin would say; of course, those were his hands – and they were huge), and a full seven feet across in the middle. It took four men and a boy to lift that boat out of the water at the end of the season.

Uncle Art called his out-board motor "the Wizard." It was almost as old as the boat, but it purred along in perfect rhythm at the powerful guiding hand of the big crippled man. The boat, the motor, and Bobby's great uncle were like one soul in that body of water.

As they crossed the lake, Bobby was up at the bow, on his knees, on the point seat. His arms were slung straight back behind him, his face forward. He looked like a hood ornament on a "41 Chevy. His short, thick, sandy hair was being tossed in the wind by the speed of the boat.

Every year, at the beginning of summer, his dad would shave Bobby's head smooth – 'for ticks." This always baffled Bobby. His sister had long, blonde hair, but they never shaved her head. And she got wood ticks on her, too. All of the *boys* he knew got the same treatment from their dads, so at least he didn't feel singled out. After the head shaving, his hair would grow out over the summer, and, right now, it was about two inches long. The lake was like a big blue mirror in front of him. People waved from both shorelines – sometimes from over a quarter mile away. They knew Art was going fishing, and probably wanted to know who the lucky boy was who got to go with him. There wasn't one fisherman on that lake that didn't admire – and envy Art's fishing prowess. He was a master. But Bobby didn't know this. His eyes were closed. He felt like he was in the back seat of his dad's convertible. All of the kids in the neighborhood – even the bullies – (especially the bullies) – would watch him drive by and wish it was their dad driving that beautiful car, and that they were Bobby – Prince of the Morris Park neighborhood.

The smooth purring of the Wizard was getting deeper. The boat was slowing down.

Bobby opened his eyes. They were entering a small bay. At the end of it was an even smaller bay, covered with lily pads. Uncle Art cut the motor. The big boat serenely sliced the water, gliding deeper into the first bay.

Bobby looked back at Uncle Art.

His great uncle smiled and said softly, "Look into the water and count what you see."

Bobby gave him a puzzled look. Uncle Art motioned for him to turn around.

Bobby was still on his knees. He leaned forward and put his hands on the bow of the boat to look into the water. The boat was still gliding, but slower now, and still slowing down. As his eyes adjusted, he started to see the bottom of the lake. It was black and ominous, and looked like it had dark clumps of hair covering it, although the water was crystal clear. The lake still had to be over twenty feet deep at this point.

As the bay rapidly got shallower, the scene changed. There were exotic plants, soft and green in color, which appeared delicate from above. Many seemed to be like wispy fingers reaching up, trying to touch the shafts of sunlight that filtered through the water.

—◦◦ ▨ ◦◦—

Bob stopped skiing as he recalled how clean and pure the lake had been.

Most lakes in the North-woods were green with algae by that time of the year, but not Lake Hanging Horn.

Maybe it was because it was spring-fed and had a high mineral content.

Maybe it was because there were no farms close to it, polluting it with fertilizer. Maybe it was just a magic lake. But, most likely, it was because it was quite cold.

Lake Superior wasn't very far away. The "Superior Lake Effect," as the locals still call it, extends past Barnum to the south, and Cromwell to the west. Lake Hanging Horn resides within that zone. Even on the Fourth of July, if the wind is coming off Lake Superior, a fog bank can develop that will cover the area with an atmosphere like chilly pea soup. On those days, the temperature won't get above forty-five degrees.

Because of that temperature range, there were fires going in the wood stoves of Great Grandpa's old log cabin every night of the summer, and they weren't just for cooking. All three stoves would be burning – the two Monarch cook stoves in the kitchen, and the big potbelly stove with the isinglass door in the big gathering room. You didn't come up to Hanging Horn without jackets and sweaters, gloves, and stocking caps.

And, of course, your fishing pole.

It's rumored that Mark Twain once said "The coldest winter I ever spent, was the summer I spent in San Francisco."

Apparently he had never been to Duluth.

But the people up there liked it that way. They were tough and hardy. And they bitched about the weather a lot – probably more than the rest of the state – but that would be a hard one to call.

Bob chuckled at the thought, gave himself an extra push with his ski poles, and let his mind return to fishing.

The lake was getting shallower. The bow of the boat was almost to the lily pads.

There was a small section – about twenty feet or so, before the lily pads, where the lake bottom was smooth and devoid of weeds.

Bobby saw gold. First in one spot. Then another. And another. He got excited, and was just about to yell out to Uncle Art that they had found gold on the bottom of the lake, when the gold began to move.

The big pan-fish with brilliantly colored underbellies of orange and yellow – and gold – were darting in every direction.

Suddenly, Bobby understood what Uncle Art had wanted him to count. In a few seconds, all of the movement was out of sight.

"Seven!" Bobby squealed with delight. "I counted seven!" He looked over his shoulder at his smiling uncle. "What are they?"

"Punkinseed sunfish." Art beamed back at him.

"Now what do we do?" Bobby asked. He could hardly contain his excitement.

"We wait."

The big green boat drifted about ten feet into the lily pads. The soft resistance brought it to a halt. They sat in silence, both of them smiling from ear to ear.

Bobby could hardly wait for whatever would happen next.

The lights of Roseland glowed across the snow in front of him.

Bob was starting to get angry. *What time did they start skiing? They couldn't have gotten to Gluek before 1:00, and I doubt that they skied after dark*, he thought. This time of year, sunset was at about 4:30 on the northern plains.

Why set up camp in the dark if you don't have to? He was beginning to question their judgment, but then he thought, *why ski across fifty miles of prairie, if you don't have to?*

He tried to think of a logical explanation for his friends actions. *It's not "really dark" until 5:30. That would give them at least three hours of skiing.* That's about how long he had been on the trail – but they had had the advantage of daylight – and each other. The guys always skied faster when they were together, than when they were alone. It was a competitive comradery. They had used this to their advantage in dozens of "citizen" cross-country ski races – such as the American Birkebeiner, the Mora Vasaloppet, and the Canadian Ski Marathon,–passing hundreds of other skiers, as a team.

They all knew each -other's strengths and weaknesses. An athletic bond had developed over decades of skiing and cycling together, allowing them to work like a well-oiled machine. Bob was usually the leader of the group – when he wasn't pissing them off.

Yeah, they would want to prove something, he thought, his anger turning into respect.

With sagging shoulders, he plodded on, while his thoughts returned to fishing.

After about ten minutes, Bobby asked Uncle Art, "What are we waiting for?"

The time had gone by quickly. While waiting, Bobby had quietly got off his knees and was sitting on the bow of the boat, facing his great uncle. The sad, silly laughter of a loon calling its mate echoed across the lake.

A Great Blue Heron was fishing along the shore, at the edge of the lily pads. Bobby watched as it caught a four inch-long fish and ate it. He had never seen anything like that before. A deer had come down to the lake to drink in a wooded area across the bay, still covered in its reddish summer coat.

Bobby was aware of everything around him. It was like he was tapped into the universe.

"We're waiting for them to come back," Art said, in a low, deep voice.

"How long does that take?" Bobby asked. He was doing his best to be curious, not impatient.

"Should be just a few more minutes." Uncle Art motioned for Bobby to come over to him.

Bobby got up slowly and quietly walked over to his great uncle. This took him several minutes. He calculated every step carefully, gingerly stepping over the three painted wooden bench seats on-to the painted wooden slats – about two inches wide and an inch apart – that formed a floor above the deep hull. The slats ran the length of the boat – from the bow, to the wooden bench seat at the stern – and had been installed there to make it easier for Uncle Art to get in and out of the boat. An opening in the slats behind the stern seat (where Uncle Art sat, operating the Wizard) allowed access to the hull, so that any collecting water could be bailed out. Even though the slats formed a nice, flat, walking surface, on one of his steps, Bobby's-right foot twisted in the space between the slats and he lost his balance. Despite a shooting pain in his leg, he slowly caught himself and finished his journey without making a sound.

Uncle Art softly nodded his head with approval as the chubby little boy in a tee-shirt and shorts sat down on the bench seat across from his great uncle, facing him.

"It's time," Uncle Art said with a smile.

The only things in the big green boat with Bobby and his great uncle were two fishing poles, the Folgers coffee can with angleworms in it, and two oars.

As Bobby looked around, it dawned on him that Uncle Art's' crutches weren't in the boat. *Maybe this is the only place that he doesn't feel crippled,* he pondered sadly.

He thought back to the other fishing trip – just that spring – with his dad and his dad's boss, and the boss's son. They had tackle boxes, minnow buckets, a gas can (on the second day), a bag of clothes that just got wet – along with them and everything else, and a large, heavy "Cronstroms" cooler that was never used.

The cooler had belonged to his dad's boss, who said it was to hold the fish they caught. The man opened it up once, in the boat, but Bobby's dad said, "Leave it." His dad's boss had slammed the cover back down and he got even crabbier after that. Bobby and the other boy had to carry the cooler once, and they both wanted to know why it was so heavy. The men had just looked at each other and Bobby's dad said "never mind."

Oh, yeah, and they had had the long-handled net that was too small for muskies.

But, in Uncle Art's boat, there were only the poles, the oars, the worms, the man, and the boy.

The fishing poles were identical. They each had an open-faced reel with fishing line that looked like thin black string.

Bobby looked at his left hand. His fresh scar went all the way across his palm. The fishing line that had given him that scar, was different than this fishing line. That other fishing line had been shiny, like a wire made of glass.

The open-faced reels that were in Uncle Art's boat, had little brass screws implanted on the outer face of bright silver metal discs which formed the sides of the reels. Each of the sides had the word "Shakespeare" engraved on them. It was in cursive, like the big kids used. Bobby thought the writing was neat, and the word stirred his imagination. He smiled and read it to himself; "Shakespeare."

Thinking about it, Bob wondered if that was why he had collected all of Shakespeare's works over the years. Even now, every once in a while he would be drawn to read one of them, (though the soliloquys drove him nuts.)

Bobby had seen the inside of Great Grandpa Martin's pocket watch once. It kind of looked like the fishing reel that he was holding in his hands. And the knobs that your fingers held to reel in the line were made of the same material as the sides of Bobby's new pearl-handled pocket knife.

Each fishing pole had a hard cork handle, just below the reel. The reel was then attached to a ham-mered steel rod – about a quarter of an inch square up by the reel – tapering down to a point at the end of its five-foot length. The eyelets that the fishing line went through were brass and were tied to the rod with thin copper wire. As with everything in and around the old log cabin on Lake Hanging Horn, the rods and reels looked very old, and felt very well made.

Bobby had grown to like that. The kerosene lan-terns, the brass beds, the hand-stitched quilts, and the cabin itself –

all of it – made you feel safe, like you belonged, and you were family. . Bobby liked his house back in the city. *But I think I like the cabin better,* he thought.

Uncle Art reached into the coffee can. Bobby reached for a fishing rod.

"Not yet," his great uncle said calmly. "We've got to make them greedy first."

Bobby wrinkled his nose and squinted in confusion. "Greedy?" he whispered.

Uncle Art had an angleworm in his hand. He tore it in half and tossed one piece into the water like he was throwing a Frisbee. It hit the water at the edge of the lily pads, about ten feet away, right where Bobby had seen the big sunfish.

In a few seconds, there was a disturbance on the smooth surface of the water. Then a small splash where the worm had gone in. Bobby watched intently.

"They're fighting over it," Uncle Art whispered.

He repeated the worm toss a half dozen times, in different directions, twice further out. He got the frenzied response only once again, close to where the first splash had occurred. Bobby looked on with eager anticipation.

"They're going back into their beds," Uncle Art said with a smile.

Bobby giggled at the thought of fish climbing into brass beds with homemade quilts. It reminded him of the TV commercial with Charlie the tuna. "Sorry, Charlie. Only the best tuna is good enough for StarKist." He and his sister would chant the slogan whenever they saw the commercial. Their eyes would meet and they would both laugh. He wished that she was with them in the boat, because he knew she would have liked this fishing trip.

Uncle Art slowly picked up a fishing rod. There was one small hook at the end of the black line. He took half an angleworm and slid it onto the hook, then folded it over and stuck it again. He repeated this several times.

Somehow, Bobby thought, *this doesn't seem disgusting. Not like shoving a wire down the throat of a minnow until it comes out its butt.*

Uncle Art pushed one of the small brass buttons on the side of the shiny reel. Holding the cork handle of the rod in his right hand, he put his right thumb on the spool of the black fishing line inside the open face of the reel. He very slowly raised the rod and reel over his right shoulder until his hand was close to his ear, and the tip of the rod was pointing straight away from his back. In a fluid motion, he swiveled the rod high over his head, and with a hard snap of his wrist he pointed the tip of the rod out in front of him. During this maneuver, he took his thumb off of the fishing line spool. The hook and worm hit the water lightly, like a leaf falling out of a calm sky, right where the first angleworm had been tossed in.

One second passed. Then two. Then three. Then – *SPLASH!*

Uncle Art's right thumb pressed back down on the spool of black fishing line inside the reel, while at the same time his wrist snapped backward, aiming the tip of the rod straight up in the air. The black line from the tip of the rod to the water went tight, and the line going into the water seemed to go crazy, cutting the surface of the water in a figure eight pattern. Art's left hand quickly, but gracefully, took control of the cork handle of the rod, with his left thumb pressing down on the fishing line spool, and the thumb and forefinger of his right hand grasping the pearl-handle knobs of the reel. He turned them half a revolution and Bobby heard a "*click*."

Art let the fishing line dart wildly across the water for a few seconds before he started reeling it in. The look on his face told Bobby that he was enjoying this immensely. A beautiful fish with a dark green back, brilliant gold and orange underside, and a large dorsal fin emerged from the water, at the end of his great uncle's fishing line. It squirmed and wriggled in the air as Uncle Art swung it over the side of the boat and let it down gently onto the slats at his feet. The captured fish flopped around ferociously.

"Whoa! Cool!" Bobby shrieked.

The entire sequence of events – from the time Uncle Art's baited hook touched the surface of the water, until the fish was in the boat, had been less than twenty seconds. Bobby had paid attention to every little detail, utterly amazed.

It was like watching his sister dance.

He had fished with his dad and those other guys for two whole days, in the cold and rain, and they never put a fish in the boat. His dad had said they got "skunked," which was another source of confusion for him. He didn't remember seeing any skunks on that trip. His dad hit a skunk once, on another trip, while they were driving with the family on their way to go camping Up North. It made the car smell really bad – "Like Pepe' Le Pew," his sister said. Despite the stink, they both laughed.

Bobby knew she would have loved to be with him here, fishing in Uncle Art's boat.

He remembered seeing her in the doorway of their house last Spring, as he and his dad left for that other fishing trip. He had felt bad for her, but what could he do?

He was only seven then, and seven-year-olds take orders, they don't give them.

Bob stopped skiing.

She was so delicate, so fun, so beautiful, he recalled. Tears streamed down his face and froze on his cheeks as he thought about his lovely sister, who had died twelve years ago. *She was a courageous fighter, but the breast cancer took her away from us much too soon.*

His brother-in-law couldn't deal with it at the end, nor could their dad. Their sadness was too deep. They just couldn't bear watching her fade away, so they said their goodbyes and went to the visiting room to wait. But Bob and their mom stayed with her. Mom fell asleep in a chair shortly after the two men left the room.

His sister woke up and smiled at him. Even though they had grown somewhat distant as they had gotten older, as adult siblings often do, they talked and laughed and shared stories of their childhood, rekindling their old bond.

Isn't that the way it usually is? Bob thought. *We let ourselves grow up and grow apart, forgetting how important we once were to each other.*

Their conversation had slowly trailed off, since she was heavily medicated for pain. And so, in the middle of a warm summer night, after God seemed to ignore all of his prayers, her hand slipped out of his and she was gone. He cried by her side until dawn. Large, silent tears.

Bob had pushed those memories out of his mind as much as he could for many years, but now, in the bleakness of this cold winter night, they all came flooding back.

He remembered how, in the morning, he had taken care of the funeral arrangements. His brother-in-law and his parents were too overwrought to be of any help, so Bob even organized the reception. His best friends – Doug, John, and Bernie – where at his side every step of the way. He couldn't have done it without them. Those are the friends you keep.

Bob gave his sister's eulogy, keeping it bright and cheerful – the way she would've liked it – with his parents looking on with solemn gratitude.

He and his friends helped carry her casket, and Bob threw the first shovelful of dirt on it, to put her into her final resting place. But he knew she wasn't really there. Her spirit was at Lake Hanging Horn, where she was a little girl again.

He saw the terrible devastation her death wreaked on their parents. They were never the same after that. He realized that children shouldn't see that kind of grief on their parents' faces, no matter how old they are. It was then that he vowed to never have kids of his own.

Bob leaned on his ski poles and hung his head, looking down at the snow.

The trail had gotten tough, but the memory of the loss of his sister was much tougher.

"She would've been a wonderful mother," he said to himself as the sadness settled over him like a lead blanket, "but it wasn't in the cards."

When she was twenty-five, she told him that she was diagnosed with infertility. It was the same condition that Uncle Art's wife, Mary, had. A few years after his sister's death, his widowed brother-in-law said that he regretted denying her wish to adopt a child. "At least then I would have someone we both had grown to love to share my life with," he had said. He still came to Bob and Linda's house for the holidays, but they could see he was a lost soul.

My wife is the one good thing that came out of that deal, Bob thought sadly.

Linda, his sister's childhood friend – and his childhood enemy – had seen the obituary in the paper, and had come to the funeral. After the reception, she asked Bob if he wanted to go out for a cup of coffee, to talk about old times. He told her that he had to help clean up, but Bernie overheard them and handed him his suit coat, saying, "We've got it covered, Chief." Doug and John nodded in agreement.

Bob and Linda talked for hours. She even got him to laugh. On the drive home, the discussion turned somber, and at one point she put her hand on his knee in support. That's when he realized that they were meant to be together. "Providence," she called it, but he knew better. The spirit of his sister brought them together.

The thought of his wife made Bob smile. He needed that. The night had grown very long, and once again, he had forgotten where he was.

He had become oblivious to the cold air that stung his frozen cheeks. He looked around, and realized that he had only skied about a mile in the last twenty minutes.

The railroad grade that he was skiing on had been elevated five to ten feet above the fields on the beginning of his journey. Now it was only two to three feet, so the snow drifts across the trail were huge. Even with the tracks left by his friends, he was often up to his knees in hard, windblown snow.

"This tour is sure putting me through it," he agonized, out loud, "I should've started it with the guys." He had all but forgotten that his car broke down in Cosmos.

At most of the road crossings, he had had to ski into a deep crevasse, some of which were as much as fifteen feet deep. These gaping "holes" in the grade had been left behind when the railroad company tore out the tracks, removing the old, dilapidated bridges with them. He had taken these in stride so far, but, adding the drifts to it was almost too much to deal with.

He was panting heavily, and the fight was almost out of him. He looked up at the stars.

They looked back at him with cold indifference.

CHAPTER 5

—◦✦◦—

B ob allowed his mind to take him back to a happier place.

Bobby looked at Uncle Art with great anticipation. "Is that a punkinseed sunfish?" he asked. His great uncle's smile told him that it was. Uncle Art picked up the fish and held it in his right hand. The pan-fish was twice as big as his hand – and his hands were huge, just like Great Grandpa Martin's. He used his thumb to hold down the large dorsal fin on the fish's back. With his left hand, he carefully removed the hook from its mouth.

"Are you gonna catch anymore?" Bobby was so excited that he could hardly sit still.

"It's your turn," Art said solemnly, looking down at the fish.

Bobby's mouth dropped open.

"I can't do that!" he said in a whisper, not really sure if that was true or not.

"Sure you can." Uncle Art's voice was patient and reassuring.

His great uncle pulled a coiled-up cable out of his vest pocket. It looked like it was coated in plastic. It had a silver metal ring that was about an inch in diameter on one end, and a shiny metal spike that was about two inches long on the other end.

"What's that?" Bobby asked.

"A stringer," Uncle Art replied.

He slipped the spike end of the stringer into an open gill of the fish until the spike came out of its mouth. Then he put the spike through the metal ring and pulled all of the cable through the fish until it was tight. He stuck the spike end into a round slot at the top of the boat transom. It was a perfect fit. Then he slipped the pumpkinseed sunfish into the water at the back of the boat, and the cable, which was about five feet long, uncoiled most of the way.

"Get your fishing pole," Uncle Art said, looking up and smiling at Bobby. He pointed to the rod leaning up against the bench seat that Bobby was sitting on.

Bobby picked up the rod gingerly. He had been trained to be careful with other people's things ever since he allegedly lost his sister's Raggedy Ann doll. He was four when that happened. He was still paying penance for it.

He looked down at the cork handle on the fishing pole. It had the initials "RC" on it.

RC, Bobby thought, *Robert Christianson*. It was Bobby's grandpa's pole. *What an honor*, he sighed. As far back as he could remember, he was relieved that he had been named after Grandpa Christianson instead of his other grandpa. That grandpa, who died before he was born, had been named Elmer. Bobby shuddered at the thought. *Just think what the kids on the playground would do with that nickname!* Bobby's dad wouldn't let him touch any of his fishing equipment. "Not yet," his dad had said. "Not until you learn how to fish with your own stuff."

So, instead, his dad gave him the Zebco fishing pole. Even though it was new, Bobby didn't like it. It wasn't as nice as his dad's rig. And the reel was enclosed, so you couldn't see how it worked. *And it can cut your hand,* he thought.

He just realized that Uncle Art had left the Zebco fishing pole back on the dock. That was a good place for it.

His grandpa's fishing pole was solid, just like Uncle Art's. It was a little heavy for him, but he could feel the balance in it. Bobby reached for an angleworm.

"Not yet," Uncle Art said, putting his hand over the coffee can. "Practice first."

Bobby had watched every move that Uncle Art had made when he caught his fish, with a concentration that was far beyond his age. He was pretty sure he could do it.

Uncle Art instructed, "Swing yer line over here." Bobby did as he was told, with a smooth sweep of the wrist that made it look like he had done this a thousand times before.

His great uncle pulled two small metal balls out of a vest pocket. Each one had a slot in it.

He slipped the slot of one of the metal balls over the fishing line just above the hook, put it in his mouth and bit down. He did the same with the second ball.

"What's that for?" Bobby cocked his head in curiosity. He hadn't seen Uncle Art put anything on *his* fishing line.

"They're lead weights, called sinkers," Uncle Art said with a calm smile. "So that your hook will weigh about the same as the angleworm." He motioned for Bobby to slide to the other side of the boat, away from where he had caught the fish. "Give it a try," Uncle Art said, beaming proudly at the little boy in front of him.

Bobby's right hand grasped the cork handle firmly. He slipped the brass button on the side of the reel and put his thumb on the spool of fishing line. He swung the rod over his shoulder just like his great uncle had done, and delivered the first cast of his life.

The hook hit the water with a loud splash right along the edge of the boat.

Bobby's heart sank. He transferred the cork handle into his left hand and reeled in the line. He was so disappointed with himself that he had to fight back the tears.

"That's okay," Uncle Art said patiently, "Try it again."

Bobby performed the same cast as before, but this time he snapped his wrist, and followed through the motion with his hand forming an arc in front of him.

The hook sailed about fifteen feet from the boat and touched the water with a light "plop." Bobby thought he was going to burst with pride. He reeled in the line.

"That's it! You've got it!" Uncle Art exclaimed. His massive shoulders bobbed in approval.

Uncle Art only made him practice casting three more times before he said, "That's good, son, you're ready to fish." Bobby's legs were twitching with excitement.

His great uncle took out his pocket knife. It looked old, but it had pearl handles, just like Bobby's knife. Uncle Art used his knife blade to pry the lead sinkers off of Bobby's line, then he put them back in his vest pocket. "Now get an angleworm," he said, giving Bobby back his line.

Bobby reached into the coffee can. There was half a worm lying right on top of the dirt and coffee grounds. He picked it up without hesitation. After the ordeal of digging the worms out from under the cabin, it didn't bother him at all to put the worm on the hook, just like Uncle Art did.

He raised his rod, and dispatched his cast. The baited hook gently hit the water about five feet from where Uncle Art's line had gone in.

"One, one thousand, two, one thousand, three, one thousand," Bobby was muttering to himself while holding his breath – his sister had taught him to count like that when they played flashlight tag by their house – "Four, one thousand," he said, though his heart was sinking, "five one – "

He didn't finish the five count. The moment seemed to freeze in time as Bobby's fishing line took off across the water, and he sat there gasping.

"Set your hook, son! Set your hook!" Uncle Art almost yelled at him, laughing. Bobby's brain raced to remember what to do. There was a soft whining sound coming from his fishing reel. He put his thumb on the fishing line spool. The unwinding line against his thumb burned a little. He pressed harder and it slowed down. Then he snapped his wrist back and the line went taut.

In a second, the fishing pole was almost torn out of his hand. It felt like there was a tiger at the other end of it! His left hand instinctively grabbed the cork handle of the rod, to help out his right hand. More line was going out of the spool.

"Set the reel, Bobby!" Uncle Art squawked "Crank it in!"

The fingers of his right hand fumbled for the knobs, found them, and turned the crank half a turn. He heard a *"click*,"–and the tugging got harder.

This fish must be ten times bigger than Uncle Art's, he thought. *It's going to tear my arms off!* He remembered the Muskie he had seen that spring on Lake Trelipee. *Won't Uncle Art be surprised!*

Bobby started reeling the line in. It was hard, but the resistance was getting to be less difficult for him to control.

He loved the feeling of the tugging at the end of the line. Now he understood why Uncle Art looked so pleased when he was fishing.

Bobby's hands were getting tired, but he didn't want the moment to end. He wanted it to last forever.

The end of the line got closer to the boat. When the line went straight down into the water, Bobby raised the tip of the rod while still reeling in. A large pumpkinseed sunfish appeared above the edge of the boat, squirming wildly.

Bobby was excited, surprised, and disappointed at the same time – after all, it had felt like a whale was on his line!

Bobby swung the fish into the boat. Uncle Art's smile couldn't have been any bigger.

His great uncle showed him how to take the fish off the hook without cutting his hands on the sunfish's sharp fins.

Bobby put it on the stringer himself. He had to hold himself back from kissing his fish before he lowered it into the water with the other one.

Bob had trudged through three large snowdrifts since the last time he had stopped, yet he'd only gone about a quarter of a mile. His toes and feet were numb. The outer calves of his legs felt frozen and stiff, while the inside of his calves were burning and tingling. His thighs ached with every diagonal ski thrust he made.

I'm going to have to stop soon, or I won't be able to set up camp, he thought.

He had forgotten that his friends had both of the tents. He had all but given up on the idea of catching up with them.

The trail loomed ahead, but he noticed the snowdrifts were rapidly diminishing, because the railroad grade was rising above the prairie again. In the landscape dotted by farm lights, he thought he could make out a grove of trees about a half a mile ahead, to the left, just off the trail. "Cover," he gasped, "I'll try to make it to that."

His exhausted body retreated to the sanctuary of his mind.

—❀—

Uncle Art and Bobby traded off catching pumpkinseeds.

Bobby got a little better each time he did it, and each catch was as thrilling as the first.

Art had always felt the same way, and was pleased that he could see the joy on Bobby's face.

Once they each had caught three fish, Uncle Art asked, "There's one left, Bob. Do you want to go again?" It was as if he was talking to his brother. Bobby looked up at him. He could see the boy in his great uncle's face. Bobby smiled, but his hands hurt and his arms were sore. It was the best he had ever felt in his life. But he knew he couldn't do it again. "No, Uncle Art," he said sadly. "You get "em."

The sun was setting into the trees across the lake. Twilight was fast approaching.

Bobby was worn out, yet he felt so full from his time in the boat with his great uncle, he could burst.

As Bob thought about it, he realized that he came close to that feeling many times later in his life, while doing a variety of other activities, but it was never quite the same as that day, in that boat, on that lake.

Uncle Art baited his hook one more time. He knew the pumpkinseed wouldn't bite once the sun went down. He wanted to catch this one last fish. He let go with the final cast. When the bait touched the water, Bobby counted out loud.

"One, one thousand, two, one thousand, three, one thousand, four, one thousand, five, one thousand, six, one thousand, seven, one thousand ..." *The baited hook must be on the bottom of the lake by now,* Bobby thought, *we're only in three feet of water...* "eight, one thousand, nine–"

The last pumpkinseed sunfish was still greedy.

Uncle Art's fishing line went tight. He took his thumb *off* of the spool.

Bobby watched as the fish took the line in a big circle out into the bay, zig-zagging as it went. The line traveled about fifty feet from the boat, but it soon came back to where it had been caught. His great uncle controlled the line, keeping just enough tension to provide a little resistance. As Uncle Art "played" with the fish, it seemed to Bobby they were forming a connecting bond. The fish, the man, and the water were in a battle of respect and survival.

This is fishing, Bobby thought. His young mind squirmed to grasp the concept. It was the first time that he had formed an abstract thought, but it wouldn't be his last. *Reeling it in is just catching a fish.* He committed the thought to memory.

After several minutes, Uncle Art coaxed the pumpkinseed up to the boat.

"We got'em all, Uncle Art!" Bobby squealed excitedly. He reached for the stringer.

"No," his great uncle said, waving his hand to stop the little boy.

Bobby watched as Uncle Art tenderly removed the hook from the mouth of the fish, lowered it into the water, and gently let it go. The fish darted down into the darkness.

"This one stays in the lake," Uncle Art said in a solemn tone. "For seed."

For a brief moment, Bobby felt like he was in Sunday School and had just learned a valuable lesson: *When you take, always give back a little.*

The sun was below the horizon now. The afterglow was rapidly surrendering to the darkness. Bobby looked around. The lake looked black and spooky, like it wanted to swallow them up.

He had been on a lake after dark once before, but he had been so tired, wet, and cold that he hadn't noticed what that lake looked like, nor had he cared.

Spots of light dotted the shadowy shoreline. One of those spots was Great Grandpa Martin's old log cabin. But which one? All of the glowing dots looked the same.

"How will we find our way home, Uncle Art?" Bobby's squeaky voice sounded anxious.

His great uncle pulled the stringer holding six beautiful pumpkinseed sunfish out of the water and laid them at his feet, next to the Folgers coffee can. He chuckled under his breath.

He felt like he knew this lake better than he knew his own body. Bobby looked at Uncle Art intensely. It was too dark for his great uncle to see his inquiring eyes.

Uncle Art looked up at the stars that were just starting to come out. He loved the sky, the heavens. "The domain of the Lord," Art's father would say, sitting in his cane chair in front of the old log cabin on clear summer nights, like this one.

Uncle Art suddenly burst out, "Look, Bobby!" He was pointing at the sky, behind the boy.

Bobby turned quickly to see that he was pointing at two shooting stars streaking across the sky, heading north, away from them. They vanished in an instant.

"God's searchlights will lead us home," his great uncle said, smiling at the thought.

Uncle Art started "the Wizard" with one pull. It purred contentedly as it pushed the big green boat across the smooth black liquid, in the direction of the shooting stars.

It looks like coffee, thought Bobby, looking down into the water.

He could hardly wait to get back to the cabin and show his sister the beautiful fish he had caught.

The next day, fog rolled in. There was a bite in the air, like it was going to snow.

"When you live in Minnesota, you're either in winter, or preparing for it," his dad said. Everyone packed up and left the old log cabin a couple of days earlier than they had planned to. Everyone except Great Grandpa Martin, that is. He was an old lumberjack, and it was the beginning of his favorite time of the year.

Later that fall, Bobby heard that Uncle Art had come down with pneumonia a few days after their fishing trip. He had gotten weaker and weaker despite his wife's loving care, and he had suffered a stroke right before Thanksgiving.

Bobby's great uncle died a month later, on Christmas Eve.

Bob's mind slowly drifted back to the present time. *He never saw the lake again,* Bob thought sadly. *Fishing lost a legend, and I lost interest. I never went fishing again.*

PART TWO

DISCOVERY
AND
DELIVERANCE

CHAPTER 6

B ob was still at the convenience store in Cosmos when Doug, John, and Bernie slipped off the windswept surface of the old railroad grade and headed for a small grove of tall pine trees. The crusty, windblown snow buried Bernie up to his waist as soon as he left the trail. Doug and John were a good four inches taller than he was, so the snow only came up to their crotches as they bounded down the embankment in hot pursuit of their tour leader.

Bernie had broken trail the entire way – so far. Based on their pace and the time spent on the trail – three and a half,–no, four hours now,–he estimated that they had skied about twenty miles since they left Doug's Explorer, a little after noon.

He did not intend to pull his comrades this far on the first day, but he really wanted to find some cover to camp in. Other than a few vacant lots next to the buildings in the towns that they had skied through, this patch of trees was the first potential windbreak they had encountered.

If they had to, they would set up camp along the edge of a town, but that was never the group's first choice. They liked seclusion, so this stand of lonely pines, at least a half mile from the nearest farmhouse, was a welcome surprise. Bernie just hoped that Bob wasn't too far behind them. This trek had not been easy. Skiing it alone and in the dark would be that much tougher.

Despite a passionate protest by Doug – "I promised him that we'd wait!" – the group had decided to hit the trail. Based on past experience, they knew that Bob might not be along for hours, but they also knew that he was very capable of catching up.

John said that Bob had probably been late on purpose, just for the challenge.

Bernie thought, *he probably did it on purpose all right, but not just for the challenge.*

John had taken his position behind Bernie as he always did on this type of tour, the tips of his skis almost touching the tails of Bernie's with every kick. Doug was always close behind John, pulling up the rear. When Bob was with them, he would usually be in front, with Bernie challenging him on every stroke.

The synchronization was awesome to watch, and they could keep it going for hours.

Doug, as their "whip man" was the only one who talked. His frequent banter – and grumbling – providing a curious motivation to the group. John and Bernie would chuckle at his incessant chatter. It kept them from thinking about their aching bodies and the miles that they had left to go. Bob usually couldn't hear it. He could only hear Bernie's hot breath bearing down on him. Or passing him.

Doug was probably the strongest skier of all of them, and was definitely in the best shape. He worked out all the time. When the group needed to win a race, he would pass the others and lead the sprint to the finish to pull his friends to victory, only to back off in the last ten meters or so, on purpose, to let one of the others finish ahead of him. His fellow skiers were always puzzled by this, but they never asked him why he did it. Doug would cross the finish line with a smirk on his face, his inner grace renewed. It was always his favorite part of the entire event.

Decades of focus and discipline had honed John's body into a well-oiled machine. Over the years, his analytical mind had imprinted his muscles with the detailed information that it took to make his movements fluid, giving him the appearance of a gliding statue. With flawless form, he made it look easy. Bernie was the bull. His Finnish heritage wouldn't let him give up – or give in. Not ever. He attacked the terrain as if he was the sole surviving Suomi warrior in battle with the entire Russian army. His short, thick legs plowed through the snow drifts like they were cotton candy. The ski poles attached to his powerful arms clawed the railroad grade, tearing it to pieces through sheer determination and grit. He knew that both Doug and John would follow him twenty more miles if he wanted to keep going. Doug's grumbling would've just gotten a little bit louder, that's all.

The three friends often wondered how Bob could not only compete with them, but usually out–performed them, both on skis and while cycling. He was a little shorter than Bernie, but weighed at least twenty pounds more than he did. They never saw

– nor even heard of – him training, and he drank. A lot. Only Bernie knew how much.

Bernie would laugh and say that Bob could because "He just knows how to do it." Neither Doug nor John ever bought that idea. They figured that Bob was just mad at the world and would do anything to prove that nobody could get the better of him.

Bernie didn't argue with them.

The long shadows cast by the tall pine trees across the glistening surface of the recently fallen snow were diminishing as the three explorers fought their way through the snow drifts into the shelter of the towering firs.

"Perfect," Bernie panted under his breath, "this will do."

They had trudged into a small clearing nestled between majestic Norway Pines.

There was barely enough room for a couple of tents–and a campfire – if they were careful.

Doug immediately started packing down the snow by criss-crossing the clearing in a sidestepping fashion. John followed right behind him, tightening it up even further. In the shelter of the trees, the virgin snow was only about two feet deep. The skiers' efforts reduced that depth to six inches or so.

Bernie took off his old Kelty backpack and removed a small collapsible shovel that was strapped to the outside of it. He scanned the campsite, found a good spot, unclipped his skis, knelt down on the back of his backpack, and dug a three-foot diameter hole through the freshly packed snow down to the frozen soil beneath it.

Having finished packing the snow in the remainder of the campsite, Doug and John had taken off their identical Camp Trails backpacks and headed off into different directions, in search of dead-fall branches and limbs.

Bernie opened a compartment in his backpack and took out two Zip-loc freezer bags. He unzipped the first one and took out a "Firestarter" – a chunk of clothes dryer lint tied to a piece of paraffin wax with a cotton string. He laid it on the frozen dirt.

Doug was already alongside him with a large handful of small branches. Bernie laid them loosely over the Firestarter like he was building a small teepee. Then Bernie opened the second freezer bag and removed a box of Diamond stick matches. He took one match out of the box, struck it, and held it in his thinly gloved hand, looking at it reverently for a few seconds as if he was deep in prayer.

Then he put the flame to the lint and paraffin and a crackling campfire appeared. John skied up with a bundle of larger branches and laid them gently next to Bernie. *One match,* he thought, *of course.* John smiled at the efficiency, as Bernie fed the fire.

Now that he had sufficiently cooled down from the rigorous exercise, Doug pulled a goose down jacket out of his backpack and put it on. The others did the same. Bernie went to John's backpack and unstrapped a thin, collapsible chrome fire grate that was fastened to the outside of it. The campers had two small gas stoves with them,–and plenty of fuel,– but they all preferred to cook over a fire, if possible. Bernie placed the grate over the flames.

They had been at the site of their evening lodging for over ten minutes and not a word had been spoken out loud. They all knew exactly what to do.

Doug and John started setting up their tent, and the bantering began.

"No, no, Doug!" John said in disgust. "That pole goes over there!"

"I don't think so," Doug replied stubbornly. "Don't tell me what to do!"

Bernie untied his Sorel snow boots from the side of his backpack and used the pack as a seat while he took off his ski boots and put the snow boots on. He shook his head and laughed.

Bernie knew they had better get supper on soon, or Doug was going to get even more disagreeable. Over the years, Doug's stomach had become the group's timepiece. It frequently dictated when they were going to stop for a snack, make a meal, or even set up camp. They had almost come to rely on it. Bernie was convinced that Doug was hypoglycemic, but Bob said that Doug just had a "whining tapeworm,"- either way, Doug could eat all day and never gain weight. John was pretty much the same way, but without the complaining. Bernie and Bob, on the other hand, were both frustrated (and thankful) that they could prob-ably ski all the way across Antarctica on a bowl of rice apiece, and they would still gain weight. The same held true for all of the shorter men they knew. Go figure.

Doug, John, and Bernie had only stopped on the trail three times since they left Doug's car – to have granola bars and water. On two of the stops, they took off their skis to wax them. Two coats of light-green glide wax furiously corked in over the Swix polar base that they had hot waxed into the bottom of their wooden skis before they left home. Three coats of Rex dark green wax was applied to the "kick" zone of their skis with the same ferocity. They would use their right arms to cork the wax into their left ski and their left arms to cork the wax into their right ski. Bob had coached them on doing this, decades ago. It allowed both arms to keep limber while using different muscles than those required for standard poling action. It was especially important while traversing flat terrain where there were no hills to give you a break from the monotonous movements of the "classic" diagonal style of cross country skiing.

None of them used the more recent popular "skating" style, even when they raced.

In future years, Doug and John would succumb to its enticing temptation of faster skiing, but Bob and Bernie never adopted it. For one thing, it didn't work while touring in deep snow. They preferred the aesthetic rituals that the traditional "classic" style of skiing had to offer – intricate waxing techniques, and the feel of handcrafted wooden skis that followed the contours of the landscape beneath your feet – *that* was the pure essence of form over function.

When Doug and John skied with Bob and Bernie in their later years, they would go back to the traditional equipment and techniques. They did this out of respect – both for the sport, and for the memory of the shared youth they had come to cherish. When the men waxed their skis, they stretched their legs and arched their backs to remain loose, stay warm, and get the most out of the time not skiing.

Someone observing them from a distance would probably laugh out loud – they looked like a small flock of Sand Hill Cranes involved in an elaborate and awkward mating ritual. Even so, all of these meticulously developed exercises had served them well over the years, frequently giving them an edge over their competition when they raced.

Doug and John's tent was up and their gear was stowed. Bernie was working on his.

"I wonder when Bob is going to get here?" Doug blurted out with a crabby voice. John and Bernie looked over at each other. They knew what this was all about. Bob had a two-pound stick of Ittel's famous summer sausage in his backpack, and Doug wanted some. He had mentioned it several times when they were skiing.

Bernie shuffled through his backpack and found another freezer bag. He opened it and took out a beef stick that had also come from Ittel's meat market in Howard Lake – which Bernie's cousin owned. Even though it was over forty miles out of town, it was the only butcher shop that any of the skiers would go to.

Bernie tossed the treat to Doug. "Here! Chew on this awhile."

Doug caught it in his gloved hands and looked up excitedly. "Thanks, Bern!" He took a big bite and asked a predictable question. "Do you have more?"

Bernie shook the bag in the firelight, taunting him. He looked over at John. "Hey, Jack! You want some?"

John glanced at Doug, smiled, and shook his head "no."

Doug looked down at Bernie while chomping on his beef stick. He squinted his eyes suspiciously and asked him, "How come you didn't take these out on the trail?"

Bernie smiled and stuffed the bag into his jacket.

John took a dented and black bottomed two-quart aluminum pot out of his backpack. He walked to the edge of the trees and filled it with clean snow and put it on the chrome grate over the fire. The snow turned to water in a few seconds. If it hadn't been winter, John would've soaped the bottom of the pot before placing it over the fire. This time of year, a rag would suffice to get the fresh soot off the bottom before putting it back in his pack. It never got totally clean.

Doug used a blue plastic cup to add more snow to the pot until the water level was an inch from the top, making many trips back to the clean snow to do so.

John gazed across the campsite, then pulled a plastic quart bottle out of his backpack and said, "It's time." A shared reflection shadowed the eyes of the three friends as they looked at the bottle. Doug smirked like he was crossing a finish line. John stared curiously at the bottle in his hand, and a wry smile formed on his lips. All of the skiers could feel the aches and pains of their aging bodies, but none of them would admit it – especially not to each other. This might help.

Bernie dug deep into his old backpack and produced a large ceramic mug. Fine cracks stained with years of coffee consumption spidered its cream-colored sides, and small chips gnarled it's brim. A faded Finnish flag graced the side of it.

The cup had been his grandfather's, kiln-fired by a relative over ninety years ago.

Doug had his blue plastic cup. It used to have the word "Mazatlan" embossed in gold on the side of it, but the letters had worn off. Ten minutes after he bought it, in a gift shop on the beach, Doug met the love of his life. Right now, she was in Arizona tending to her mother.

John had a wooden goblet, which he had discreetly carved in Mr. Lund's woodworking shop back in junior high school. Even though it was damn near perfect, he never got a grade on it. It wasn't something that you were supposed to make in class. The object represented one of the few times in his life that he had not followed the rules. He carried the cup – and the memory with a defiant pride.

John poured a couple of ounces of amber-colored liquid into each of their chalices.

"Bob should be here," he said soberly. The others nodded in agreement.

Doug remembered the sausage stick. "What if he doesn't come?" he asked anxiously.

"Has he ever *not* done anything that he said he was going to do?" John replied coldly.

Doug turned away and shook his head "no."

Bernie held his mug up in a toast. "To the Trail," he said with reflection.

The others raised their cups. "To the Trail," they whispered in agreement.

Bernie sipped his drink slowly, savoring all of it. He looked at John and smiled.

"Talisker?" he queried. John smiled and snorted. "Amazing! How did you know?"

Bernie gave him a sly look, finished his drink and put his sacred cup back into his backpack, burying it deep to keep it safe. He thought about telling John that he had seen the empty bottle of single-malt Scotch sitting on the counter when they picked him up that morning, but he decided against it. It was too much fun letting John think that he could identify the brand just by tasting it. Maybe he would tell him later.

His companions downed their Scotch and the arguing resumed. It was Doug's turn.

"That drawstring's not tight enough! If the wind comes up, it'll blow our tent away!"

"No it won't," John replied defensively, walking over to the rope and tying it tighter.

Bernie looked down at the pot of water on the fire. *It'll be at least thirty minutes before it's hot,* he thought. *I've got some time.*

He zipped up his goose down jacket and started walking in the direction of the Luce Line Trail.

"Where are you going?" John asked, putting a hold on his banter with Doug.

"No place," Bernie responded, without turning to face him.

Doug and John looked at each other and nodded. They knew where he was going.

Bernie followed the ski tracks they had made earlier, taking him away from the flickering shadows of the campsite. His eyes slowly adjusted to the dimmer light. The air beyond the grove of trees felt colder, harsher. His snow boots slipped as he made his way up the steep embankment to the top of the old railroad grade. A shiver ran down his spine, as he slowly looked both ways down the trail. To the east, a universe of stars were already gleaming against the ebony background, while to the west, a soft orange glow was fading on the horizon. Various shades of purple were above the glow – lighter in color closer to the horizon, fading into darkness as it blended into the night sky. Bernie strained his eyes in the direction of the sunset.

This vast region of prairie extended all the way to the Black Hills of South Dakota, then beyond to the Rocky Mountains. He watched as the western sky turned black, hardly breathing until the vacuum of silence was shattered by his friend's voice.

It was Doug. He was standing below Bernie, on the edge of the Norway Pines.

"Hey, Bernie! The water's hot! C'mon and eat."

Bernie broke his trance to look down at Doug. In the dim light, Bernie couldn't see his smile. Doug turned to look off into the western twilight, then turned back to face the dark shape of Bernie standing on the old railroad grade.

"Don't worry, Bern. He's comin'," Doug said softly. His voice was uncharacteristically soothing.

"No. No, I don't think so," Bernie muttered under his breath. "Not yet."

Doug looked over his shoulder at the campsite. His voice quickly returned to normal, "C'mon, pal! The kettle's on the boil!" He waved his arm to draw Bernie in.

The motion was futile. Bernie couldn't see it against the dark backdrop of the trees.

Bernie looked back to the west, squinting to see into the darkness.

Doug tried to get Bernie off the railroad grade again. "C'mon man! It's been a long day!" He snorted loudly and threw his hands up in the air in disgust. He was getting desperate. He knew that John wouldn't let them start eating until all of them were together. On the trail, they said a prayer before dinner. It was one of John's many rules.

Doug yelled, "Damn stubborn Finlander," loud enough for Bernie to hear it. "I'm hungry".

Doug turned and walked back to the campsite, his stomach grumbling. A terrible thought occurred to him: *John better not make us wait for Bob!*

Bernie watched Doug disappear into the trees. "I s'pose I better go," he sighed.

He took one more look down the trail to the west and yelled back at Doug. "His wife is going to kill us if we let him freeze to death out there."

He smirked at the impatience of his companion, "Doug and his appetite," he whispered.

Bernie was just about to follow him back into camp when he heard a faint sound to the southeast of him. He turned to see the dim headlights of a car, west-bound on Highway 7, about five hundred feet away. For some reason that he couldn't explain, his eyes were drawn to it. *That's odd,* he thought. As the vehicle passed him, he noticed a weird amber glow surrounding it. The strange aura illuminated the car. He watched the taillights until they disappeared from view. "It looks like an old Cadillac convertible," he muttered to himself.

A chill went down his spine. The words, "Now Bob's coming," appeared in his mind.

Bernie smiled until the ice crackled in his frozen mustache. He laughed out loud as he slid off the railroad grade and trotted into camp to put some hot stew in his belly.

CHAPTER 7

The memories of his great uncle, the old log cabin, and the loss of his sister had worn Bob to a frazzle, and the bitter cold of the January night was working its way into his soul. Sharp pangs of nostalgia rippled through him as the heat escaped his body with every breath he took.

He felt spent and so very alone.

Despite his better judgment, Bob sat down in the snow, leaning back against his backpack. He put his head between his knees and wrapped his arms around them. His ski pole straps dangled limply from his wrists. His mind was in a fog and he was panting heavily.

He felt like going to sleep. Right there, on the trail, right now.

He fell on to his side. *So this is what it's like when you finally give up,* he thought, as he began to doze off. For the first time since he'd gotten out of the Cadillac, he started to feel warm all over, as if he was lying on a summer beach with the hot fingers of the sun reaching for his body.

Just as he started to fall asleep, he thought he heard a voice calling his name.

It sounded like Uncle Art.

Bob opened his eyes, looking up at the stars. The murky haze that had dominated his conscious thoughts for most of this journey seemed to melt away, as the bitter cold creeping through his clothing brought him a new, heightened sense of awareness. Bob slowly scanned the fields on either side of him, straining to see further into the darkness. "It can't be," he muttered to himself in a hoarse whisper. "He's dead."

He stood up, shaking himself off. Without snow drifts, he had skied faster, covering more distance. Bob looked down the trail in the direction he was headed. "Son of a bitch," he mumbled.

For the first time that night, his friends' ski tracks were not in front of him.

"Son of a bitch!" he yelled much louder, "I skied right past them!"

He spun around. Sure enough, there was only one set of tracks behind him.

"*Dammit!* I could already be in camp!"

He quickly forgot that, moments before, he had been lying in the snow, ready to quit.

Now he didn't want to sleep. He didn't even want to drink. He just wanted to finish for the night.

He had gone at least a half mile past the grove of trees he had seen earlier. Since he knew they hadn't gone farther, he was sure that his friends were camped there. If possible, they would've found a secluded place out of the wind, just in case it came up.

He turned around and started skiing back the way he came. His glide and his kick were both gone. His weary legs could only take him about a foot at a time. "I should re-wax," he muttered, but the thought of taking off his skis, – and putting "Old Gerry" back on again after he was done, – was agonizing. Besides, it wasn't that far to go.

He just wasn't used to having equipment that didn't perform better than he did.

"I'll make it," he said wearily. He let out a heavy sigh and redoubled his efforts.

Suddenly, his tired eyes caught movement. Low in the sky, right in front of him, a light burned across the heavens, from north to south. Then another, and another.

It became a full-blown meteor shower.

"Wow!" he gasped. "I wouldn't have seen this if I hadn't gone too far." He momentarily forgot his exhaustion. The sight was mesmerizing.

The shooting stars lit up the night – and the surface of the snow in front of him.

He diverted his eyes from their brilliance, feeling oddly unworthy of the beauty.

Bob cast his gaze across the snow, and spotted a large black disc, roughly four feet in diameter, lying on the surface of the snow, about forty feet in front of him. It was on the north side of the railroad grade, down the embankment. The top of it was about three feet below the trail he was standing on.

Curious, he ground his skis forward on the grade until he was perpendicular to it. Now the object was only about fifteen feet away, directly below him.

It looks like the roof of a car, he thought, *but that doesn't make any sense. The Luce Line isn't a road.* The last road that he had crossed, back to the west, was over a mile away, back in the deep snow drifts, where the grade was about the level of the fields.

Before he had turned around to go back toward the grove of trees, he hadn't seen any lights crossing the grade to the east – not for as far as he could see, anyway. No lights that would indicate that there was a road crossing the trail.

All the roads that he had crossed that night, from State Highway 277 where he had been dropped off, to the county roads, even the farm driveways, had some lights on them. At times they were over a thousand feet apart, but it was enough to identify a road.

About a half mile to the north, he saw the dim lights of a farmhouse and a barn. He could barely make out a line of plowed snow, leading to the west from the house.

Bob looked down at the black disc in the snow, and cocked his head as he pondered.

It must be the roof of an abandoned car. Farmers often do that. They haul cars and other equipment they don't want out to the edge of their fields. He nodded his head in confirmation. *Yeah, that's what it is.*

The reflection of two more shooting stars briefly shot across the shiny black surface, and it shimmered with a strange iridescence. He thought his eyes were playing tricks on him. Frost was covering his eyebrows and eyelashes. He rubbed his eyes with the back of his gloved hand, and looked again. The reflection of another meteor flashed across its' surface. This one was brighter. The black object seemed to come alive with an eerie glow that was not of this world.

"Wow! Would'ya look at that," he said, in a coarse whisper.

He felt compelled to go down to the disc, but then it occurred to him, *It's off the trail, the snow must be at least six feet deep down there.*

It would be a waste of time – and energy, and he didn't have much of that left.

But he was drawn to it.

He watched as the points of his skis moved in the direction of the object, as if his feet didn't belong to him. His skis slipped off the grade and started down the embankment.

Instantly, he was up to his waist in snow. Gravity was pulling him slowly forward, but the snow was providing major resistance. With his ski poles still clinging to his wrists by their straps, and dragging along the surface of the snow, he used his hands and arms to pull himself forward. It was like he was standing up, dog paddling in the snow. Bob was soon buried up to his armpits in the white stuff.

I could've taken my backpack off on the grade! He threw his head back at the thought, agonizing over the lack of planning. *It's gonna be really hard to get back outta here. What was I thinking?* The reality of his situation was settling in. The bottoms of his skis were at least four feet below the surface of the snow, and it would be very hard to turn them around or to take them off.

The tips of his skis hit something hard, just before his hands reached the disc. *Yeah, of course it's a junk car, what else would it be?* He thought, disgusted with himself over his own foolishness. *The guys are gonna get a good laugh over this one.* He knew that the next day the group would ski right by there and see the tracks going off the trail. With no other skiers out on this part of the Luce Line, it would be pretty hard for Bob to say that they weren't his tracks.

Bob let out a heavy sigh, and began to dig at the snow in front of him, pushing it off to his sides.

His weary mind was picturing his warm sleeping bag, as he muttered, "Got to get to my sk – "

Bob heard a soft pounding sound and stopped digging. He cocked his head to listen.

"No way," he said out loud.

There it was again. It was coming from beneath the black disc in front of him.

"Oh my God!'

He forgot about the cold. He forgot about how tired he was. He forgot that he was up to his neck in snow. He tore off his ski poles and started digging furiously next to the object. The powder snow under the windblown crust made for slow progress.

He finally exposed a window, covered with frost.

Then, the top of a door, then a mirror, then a black door handle. He tried to pull the handle up, but it was frozen. In a frenzy, he yanked on it harder. His fingers slipped off.

"Goddammit!" he howled, as pain shot through his hands. He went after it again.

Stop! He came to his senses. *Just stop.* He consciously started to calm himself down.

He was panting hard. His heart felt like it was going to blow out of his chest.

There's still a bunch of packed snow around the door.

Bob paused a moment to catch his breath. He heard more pounding, a little louder now. He resumed digging as fast as he could. *I'd give anything for Bernie's shovel!* his mind screamed, as he pawed at the snow. It was collapsing around him as fast as he could dig it out.

It took a couple of minutes, but he got the entire door exposed. It was lighter in color than the roof. It looked like the passenger-side door of a minivan. He thought he could hear a muffled voice inside. He yanked at the door handle like a madman.

"Goddammit!" he yelled again, screaming in frustration. He leaned forward, up against the door, and tried to reach the back pocket of his old woolen knickers. His backpack was in the way. He tore off the pack, and threw it in the snow next to him.

The pocket zipper in his old woolen knickers was stuck.

"Son of a bitch!" he howled at the top of his lungs. His anger echoed across the frozen landscape. He could probably be heard in Hutchinson, forty miles away.

Bob tore the zipper open, breaking it. He reached in and got out an old pearl-handled pocket knife and snapped it open. The blade was half its original size, worn down by a little sharpening and a lot of heavy use. Over the years, he had used it for everything from scraping the paint off his house trim, to stirring his coffee.

He had just found a new use for it.

He jammed the knife blade into the rubber seal between the top of the door and the roof of the van. He did this over and over again, at about two-inch intervals. Once, the blade closed in on the knuckle of his little finger of his right hand. He yelped in pain as it crunched the bone under the thin, leather ski gloves.

Bob tore off his gloves and threw them at his backpack and tried to get his fingers into the space at the top of the door.

"Not enough room," he snarled, his angry voice reflecting off the frosty glass window.

He put the pocket knife in his left hand and began jabbing at the rubber seal. The blade collapsed again, this time on the palm of his hand, right on his old fishing line scar. The dull blade cut deep. Blood started dripping in the snow almost immediately.

"Piece – a – shit!" he screamed, mostly in embarrassment for letting the knife do that to him. He knew it didn't have a locking blade. He tried to look at his cut, but the light was too dim to see much. He put his ski glove back on that hand to stop the bleeding.

Wait a minute, he thought. *What am I doing? Why don't I just break the window?*

Bob reached across the snow and grabbed his backpack. He knew there was a hatchet buried in there somewhere. He unzipped the top compartment of the pack and dug through the contents with his right hand, feeling his way past freezer bags with rice, pasta, jerky, a stick of summer sausage, and a plastic bottle full of undiluted scotch. His little finger was throbbing in pain as his hand closed in on the thin, wooden handle of the hatchet. He yanked it out, took off the leather sheath, and raised it to hit the window when a deep voice called out, "What's goin' on down there?"

Bob spun around in total surprise. He hadn't heard another voice in the last several hours. His hip bumped the old pocket knife that was stuck in the rubber between the car door and the frame. The blade broke off, still in the rubber. The pearl handle fell and disappeared into the snow at his feet.

Bob looked up into the star-studded blackness.

The silhouette of a man was visible on the old railroad grade.

CHAPTER 8

―ↄ✸ↄ―

B ob snapped out of the trance he had been in since finding the car.

He knew that voice all too well.

"Bern!" he called out to his friend. "I need your help!"

Bernie snapped out of his skis, dropped his poles, and waded down to Bob.

"Where's Doug and John?" Bob asked Bernie.

"They're comin'. They were already in the sack. I was sitting by the fire readin' when I heard the yellin'. Thought someone got caught in a bear trap or somethin'. When I finally figured out it was swearing, I knew it was you."

Bob threw a glare at him. "I don't curse that much."

"Yeah, right," Bernie replied sarcastically.

"Readin'?" Bob said, matching Bernie's sarcasm. "Don't tell me. *The Cremation of Sam McGee.*"

Bernie smiled in the darkness. *It's good to have friends who know you so well.*

He got alongside Bob. "So what the hell are ya doin' down here?" he asked.

"There's somebody in this car," Bob said solemnly.

109

Bernie's eyes got big. "You're kidding me?" he gasped.

Bernie looked deep into Bob's eyes. Even in the half-light he could see they meant business.

Both men jammed their fingers into the top of the door.

Bob had forgotten about the hatchet. He had dropped it when Bernie startled him.

The two pulled as hard as they could. They heard the sound of crackling frost. The door was starting to break free of the ice that bound it.

"Pull up on the handle," Bob grunted.

Bernie pulled the handle with his left hand, while he was still pulling on the door with his right hand. Both men growled loudly, giving it all they had. The door swung about halfway open.

A billow of steam escaped from the open door, and, with it, a noxious odor.

Bernie smelled it first, and started to gag, covering his face with the back of his hand. He backed away from the vehicle.

The stench hit Bob. It was overpowering.

Somebody died in there, Bob thought, coughing. *And not very long ago.*

The dome light came on dimly as Bernie pushed the door open farther, moving a foot of snow with it. A woman was sitting in the driver seat of the minivan. Her skin was yellow and had a dull, damp, shine to it. The air inside the van was warm and humid, thick and nauseating.

"She's dead," Bernie said sadly. Bob nodded his head in acknowledgment.

In all of the commotion, he had forgotten about the pounding sounds he had heard.

The woman slowly turned her head and opened her eyes to look at them.

The men were so startled, they almost jumped out of their knickers.

"What are you two assholes doing down there?" It was Doug's sarcastic voice.

Both of the men jumped at the sound of a new voice. Bob looked up on the grade. The forms of two tall men were standing there, leaning on their poles. John had on a headlamp

"It's a woman. She was trapped in the snow. We thought she was dead, but – ", Bob realized what he was saying. *How callous could he be? She was sitting right there!*

"She's alive." Bernie finished the sentence. "But she's sick. Go get help!"

"What?" asked Doug. He was momentarily confused by the startling development. His sleepy mind tried to grasp the situation. "Where do we go for help?"

"The farm house!" Bernie responded, pointing to the dim lights north of them.

John finally joined the conversation. "No. We'll go to Blomkest. It's only a couple miles. It'll be a lot easier skiing." He remembered the snow drifts they had skied through, back on the trail near Roseland. It looked the same toward the farm house.

Bob and Bernie looked at each other and nodded in approval. Bernie smiled at John.

Always the thinker, Bernie thought. The rest of the group usually just dove into action and did things without thinking about it. But not John. He always took the time to figure out a better way. If you want to create a perfect crew, put your bull workers with a thinker.

Doug and John took off to the east in the best racing form they could muster on a trackless, wind-blown trail. As Bob and Bernie watched them fade out of sight, they heard John talking, "Remember, Doug? We drove through Blomkest looking for a convenience store. There was a fire station there."

"Oh yeah," Doug responded. "But it's probably volunteer out here."

"Then we'll knock on doors," John replied.

"Yeah," Doug's voice became excited at the thought. "All of "em if we have to."

The woman mumbled something.

"What should we do until they get back with help?" Bob asked Bernie.

He was beat. He couldn't think straight anymore. He knew he had to rely on Bernie.

"It's all right. You're going to be okay," Bernie said to the woman in a deep, soothing voice. "We found your car buried in the snow –". Bernie stopped midsentence and looked over at Bob with a furrowed brow. "How did you find this car? You skied right past us. Didn't you see our tracks turning off the trail?" Bernie was more than a little curious.

Bob had known this was coming. No matter what he said, it wouldn't make any sense.

"I was daydreaming," he said sheepishly.

Bernie was a practical man, and he knew Bob to be one too. No bullshit. No messing around. If you wanted to see that kind of behavior, you turned to Doug, the joker.

"Daydreaming?" Bernie snorted. "Out on these snowdrifts, after dark, below zero? About what?"

It didn't compute. He knew Bob could be quiet and brooding sometimes, but daydreaming? Was he drunk? Hypo-thermic? Or just going senile?

"Fishing," Bob replied. He looked wistfully out across the fields. "Fishing," he muttered again.

"Fishing?" Bernie laughed. "You don't fish." Now he was really confused.

"A long time ago." Bob turned to glare at him. "What is this, fifty questions?"

Bernie caught the intensity in his eyes and decided it was time to drop it. He knew he'd find out eventually. But Bob daydreaming about fishing? Weird.

"Wendy," the woman whispered feebly.

Bernie diverted his attention back to her. She was trying to raise her right arm.

Bernie crawled across the passenger seat to comfort her. "Don't worry, Wendy," he said, "we won't leave you. We'll stay right here until the cavalry comes."

She slowly shook her head from side to side. Bernie noticed her lips were parched.

"Got any water?" he asked Bob.

Bob reached over and pulled his old backpack across the snow toward himself. He unzipped a compartment and hesitated as he handed Bernie the container.

Bernie took the plastic water bottle and unscrewed the top to give the sick woman a drink.

"Jesus Christ, Bob," he said disgustedly.

Bob shrugged his shoulders. "Now who's swearing?" he retorted sarcastically.

Bernie's nose had caught a strong whiff of Scotch in the water. He knew that Bob drank way too much, but he had never seen him drink on the trail before.

"I thought you told Linda you were going to cut back on this?" Bernie wasn't happy. He had promised Bob's wife that he would try to keep a tight rein on Bob's drinking. Marrying Linda was the best thing that ever happened to Bob, and Bernie didn't want to see him screw it up. Bernie only wished he could find a woman as fine as her. After years of looking, he'd all but given up, but he knew she was out there, somewhere. And here was Bob, being stupid. He ought to smack him one.

Bob was looking down into the snow. Bernie could be like his dad sometimes. Except Bob's dad never drank. Ever. Bob's dad had grown up with a mean, alcoholic father and knew that alcohol addiction ran rampant in his family. His sobriety didn't stop him from being a hard-ass, though. Unfortunately, Bob inherited both negative qualities. It didn't make him a bad person, just a difficult one to be with,–sometimes.

Bob looked up. "You won't tell her, will you? I didn't have that much in the car."

"Is this why you didn't ride with us?" Bernie was giving him "the inquisition."

"No. I had to put together a demo bid." Bob looked at him sincerely. "Really."

Bernie turned away and leaned into the van with the Scotch and water bottle.

"Wait a minute!" Bob grabbed Bernie's arm. "That's twelve-year-old Glenlivet in there."

Bernie sighed and shook his head in disgust, handing Bob the water bottle.

Bob took a long swig and handed it back to his friend. "Have some," he pleaded.

"C'mon, Bern," Bob continued with a sly grin, "You won't want any after she's had a drink." Bob pointed over at the woman. "Look at her, she's sick."

Bernie was just about to tell Bob how disgusting he was, when he saw the look on Bob's face. Bernie shrugged his shoulders and took a long drink from the water bottle. When he was done, Bernie smiled at Bob and said firmly, "Don't tell Linda, okay?"

Bob smiled back at him, relieved. "Okay".

Bernie climbed back into the van to give the woman a drink.

Bob was still smiling. He knew Bernie wasn't lying when he said that he was reading by the campfire. But that wasn't why he was still awake. Bernie was waiting for him to show up.

Bernie was probably just on the verge of putting on his skis and looking for him when he heard the swearing. Bob knew that Bernie would've skied all the way back to the start of the trail, if it was warranted. Bob would do the same for him, if the tables were turned.

Bob's dad used to say they were "connected at the hip." Bob had met Doug and John years before he met Bernie, back when they were ten. That's when he moved into the "new" neighborhood with his mom and dad and his sister. Despite his shyness and insecurity, he had quickly become friends with the two boys who lived on his block, but he was never as connected to Doug and John as they were with each other. Their unspoken bond was like Bob and Bernie's. Collectively, though, they had become family. Bernie was on his knees on the passenger seat of the mini-van. He looked down and saw an empty ceramic coffee cup sitting on the center console of the Ford Aerostar.

"This might be easier," he muttered to himself. He poured a few ounces of the alcohol–enriched water into the cup. "Besides, Bob will need a chug or two off the water bottle in the morning." He'd rather see Bob do that, than go for the undiluted scotch container that he knew was lingering in Bob's backpack.

Bernie stuffed the plastic water bottle into his own jacket and picked up the coffee cup.

It was covered with a gooey substance. He looked closer at the dashboard. It was covered, too, as was the steering wheel and the front of the woman.

"It's puke!" he whispered in disgust, suddenly getting very nauseated. He scrambled backwards out of the van, still holding the coffee cup.

He looked over at Bob, who was pulling a down vest out of his backpack.

Bob looked up at him and shivered. "It's getting colder out here." He put on the vest. "Did you get her to drink?" Bob saw the coffee cup and realized that his water bottle wasn't going to get contaminated after all. He pointed at it, smiling. "Thanks, Bern."

"She won't drink for me," Bernie said. "But I'll bet she'll drink for you."

In the dim light, Bob couldn't see that Bernie's face was whiter than the snow, and sweaty. Bob looked into Bernie's eyes and dropped his smile. "Oh, no," he replied. "I supplied the water. It's your job to give it to her." He had seen what it looked like in the van. And he knew what that smell was, too. He had woken up next to it many times.

Bernie looked serious.

In desperation, Bob blurted out, "Your mom's the nurse."

Bernie snapped out of his nausea. "What the hell is that supposed to mean?!"

"Well, you know," Bob stammered, "She trained you for this kind of stuff."

Bernie shook his head in denial. "No she didn't." He was lying. His mom had taught her kids all kinds of first aid and nursing techniques. He had known how to set a broken bone since he was five years old. His mom always wanted him to get into the medical field. She knew he had the temperament for it, but he didn't have the stomach. "You should at least marry a nurse," she would tell him. Nothing would make her happier.

Bernie knew that Bob had won the argument, as he usually did, so Bernie took a deep breath and climbed back into the van.

He put the coffee cup up to the woman's lips, but she kept brushing it away, feebly saying, "Wendy, no, Wendy."

Is she repelled by the smell of the scotch in the water? thought Bernie. *That seems unlikely, the*

*stench in this van is so bad, she couldn't possibly
smell anything else.*

"Mom could get this woman to drink Tabasco
sauce," he said to himself.

He was getting frustrated. He knew she needed
water, so why was she being so stubborn? And why
did she keep saying "Wendy'" over and over again?
Was she just delirious?

The simple explanation dawned on him. He drew
back from her. She wasn't Wendy. There was someone
else in the car. Bernie looked into the back of the van.
The dome light cast shadows on piles of clothes.

"Bob!" he called out, looking over his shoulder. "I
think there's someone else in here!"

Bob had been trying to take off his skis, which
were buried in the snow under him. He'd gotten one
boot free of the binding and was working on the other.

The snow was like quicksand down there. The
harder he struggled, the deeper he sank.

Bob looked up at Bernie and read his thoughts.

"Could that be the '"Wendy"' she keeps mum-
bling about?"

"I don't know," Bernie replied. "Maybe. I think so."

With a lot of grunting and groaning, Bob got his
other boot free of the ski binding.

"Did you get her to drink yet?"

"No," Bernie responded in frustration. He was
almost getting impatient with her.

Bob did not want to go into that car, but somebody needed to get the woman some water, and given the choice between doing that and rummaging through the van, he would choose the latter. "Move over, Bern. I'd better take a look," he said reluctantly.

"It's pretty dark back there," Bernie said nervously. He almost sounded afraid.

Bob unzipped three compartments in his backpack until he finally found a small flashlight. He didn't like using them, but he knew Linda always snuck one in, probably while looking to see how much liquor he was bringing with him. Tonight he was glad she did. The thought of his loving wife made Bob smile, inspiring him to sing a song that always reminded him of her – "Up on Cripple Creek, she sends me, if I spring a leak…" Bernie heard the familiar lyrics and joined in …"she mends me, I don't have to speak, she defends me…"

The sick woman looked over at Bernie and managed a weak smile. She knew the song too. She took a big drink from the coffee cup.

Bernie backed out of the van, and gave Bob a piercing glare while finishing the lyric "…a drunkard's dream, if I ever did see one ……"

He pointed his finger at Bob. "You got that right. Don't mess it up."

Bob gave him his innocent "Who, me?" look and climbed into the van.

He turned on his flashlight, diverting it so it wouldn't shine into the eyes of the woman.

With more light, he noticed the driver's side window was down about an inch.

That would make a decent air hole, he thought.

On the center console, over the van's engine, there was a pack of cigarettes, a crumpled potato chip bag, a bean bag ashtray overloaded with cigarette butts, a Minnesota state highway map that was folded open, and the white ceramic coffee cup that Bernie had used to give her a drink, which had the word "Monet" written on it, in baby blue letters, in the style of the artists' signature.

Bob crawled across the passenger seat and shined his light into the darkness. The center seats had been taken out. There were piles of clothes on the floor and on the bench seat at the back of the van. It looked like the car was being used as a shelter, not a vehicle. What looked like large picture frames were stacked up against the wall of the van, behind the driver's seat. There were about a dozen of them. They looked like they held cardboard.

He squirmed his way between the two front seats and onto the clothes on the floor.

The odor in there was terrible, but he could take it. He and Bernie had worked in a nursing home while going to Dunwoody, the trade school where they met. They had worked the night shift to make more money. Some places in that nursing home smelled like this.

"Hello! Anybody in here?" Bob called out. This seemed redundant. If anyone was alive back there, they would've heard him and Bernie talking a long time ago. Bob reached back and handed Bernie a quilt that he found on the floor. Bernie gently tucked it around the woman as the cold outside air was creeping in-to the vehicle.

Bob climbed in deeper. He got to the bench seat and found that it was covered with coats, clothes, and a few woolen blankets. He looked behind the seat. The only thing there was a folded-up wheelchair. Puzzled, he backed away. *Was the woman handicapped?*

"Bern!" he yelled over his shoulder.

"Yeah. What?!" came the reply. "Don't yell! I'm right here." Bernie was sitting in the passenger seat, humming the rest of "Cripple Creek." It seemed to soothe the woman.

"Are there handicap controls around the driver's seat?" Bob asked.

"What? What are you talkin' about?" Bernie looked back at him.

"You know, arm controls for the pedals. Up by the steering wheel."

Bernie didn't even look. "Not that I can see." He would've noticed them before this.

Bob leaned forward to look over the seat again. He put his left hand on top of the clothes on the seat to steady himself. When he pressed down, the pain from the knife cut shot up his arm, and he quickly pulled it away. But in the brief time that his hand was on the seat, he thought he felt something different under the clothes.

It felt like the leg of a person.

He set his flashlight on top of the wooden frames to the right of him, and started pulling the clothes and blankets off the seat slowly, carefully, like he was peeling back the petals on a fragile flower.

The form of a small body lying down on the seat appeared. Thickly stockinged feet. Faded blue jeans

121

with colorful designs embroidered on the pockets. The bottom of a knitted woolen sweater. He pulled back a nylon jacket that was loosely laid over the top of the body, and peeled off a red bandana handkerchief lying flat under that.

A thin angelic face appeared, softly illuminated by the indirect glow of his flashlight. It was a beautiful little girl with silky, long blonde hair. She was about ten.

He gasped and drew back in shock and horror.

It was his sister.

CHAPTER 9

D oug and John had made it to Blomkest in less than fifteen minutes—a pretty amazing time, considering the windblown snirt they were skiing on. They skied down silent streets for a couple of minutes without seeing a light in a window, so they decided to just knock on a door.

It took another minute before the porch light came on.

A man, about sixty, with thick gray hair, a white tee-shirt, and blue pajama bottoms, came to the door. He looked through the glass at the two unfamiliar faces.

"Call the sheriff, Dottie," he said to his wife with a stern tone. "Now."

He reached down alongside the refrigerator and picked up his rifle. A Ruger .223 he had for varmints. He kept it loaded by the door in the wintertime. He used it to plug the occasional coyote that would forage by the grain elevator across the street from his house. He wasn't supposed to discharge a firearm in town, but nobody wanted them varmints around, and he knew that *nobody* would turn him in.

Tonight he might bag a couple of varmints of a different kind.

"What do you want?" he yelled through the door.

"We need an ambulance," John yelled back.

"Why? Where's the car wreck?" It was an obvious question. State Highway 7 ran by the town. Accidents happened occasionally, especially late at night, after the local bars closed.

"It's not a wreck," John responded. "We found a car buried in the snow with a woman in it. She's sick and needs some medical attention."

The man pondered a moment. It sounded believable. He had helped dig out at least a dozen cars himself in the last few days. "Where's the car?" the gray-haired man asked.

"On the Luce Line Trail," was John's reply.

"Where?" the man in the house asked suspiciously. The Luce Line crossed many roads out here, but all the ones near town had been plowed out. "At which road?"

Doug had decided to get into the conversation. "About two miles west of town. There's a small grove of trees by it."

Doug's voice wasn't as convincing. It had a certain ring to it. The gray-haired man had a cousin with a voice like that. That guy could tell you "the sky is blue," on a clear sunny day, and you still wouldn't believe him. His cousin was a smart-ass.

The older man knew every inch of the Luce Line for at least ten miles in each direction. There was no crossing where these guys were talking about. He looked at the clock above the stove. It was 12:15 a.m. He swore under his breath and got angrier.

"You boys go home and sleep it off!" he yelled through the door. "Get out of here before the sheriff gets here, or I'll put a hole through you!" He raised the gun up to the window.

John and Doug weren't deterred. They were from the city. They knew that people that threatened to hurt you seldom did. It's the ones that *don't* that you have to watch out for.

John didn't like being threatened.

For Doug it was a daily occurrence.

They both knew they were wasting valuable time. When Bernie had told them to get help, he was serious. They had heard that tone in his voice before. It meant no messing around. It wasn't John's nature to get mad, but this guy was getting to him.

"We'll knock on every goddamn door if we have to!" he yelled back, but then got a better idea. "Or we'll wait right here on your porch for the sheriff to come!"

He was calling the old man's bluff. He knew this guy wouldn't shoot them, and he was pretty sure the sheriff hadn't been notified. He needed to get this operation rolling. Right now.

Aren't the people in a small town supposed to be friendly? he thought, disgustedly.

The man glared at him through the glass. *"I'm just not going to get rid of these two, am I?"*

Despite his better judgment, he unlocked the door, still holding on to his rifle. He knew that long winters can do strange things to people. Hopefully, these guys weren't a couple of whackos. He'd hate to get blood on his new kitchen floor.

No matter what, there would be hell to pay with Dottie. She didn't like strangers in her house.

Doug and John stepped into the kitchen.

The gray-haired man looked the strangers up and down. They each had on knickers and high woolen socks with funny-looking shoes. Doug had on a burnt orange down vest, John just had on a wool sweater with a Swedish flag pattern knitted into it. The skiers took off their stocking caps and thin leather gloves when they entered the room.

"They don't look very threatening," the man snickered to himself, *"In fact, they look pretty funny."* He had to bite his lip to keep from laughing out loud.

He kept his gun pointed at them, from the hip, just the same.

It might help him with Dottie, later.

The man's wife came through the dining room door into the kitchen wearing a quilted robe and pink slippers. She had a cordless telephone in her right hand, and a small address book in the other.

"Rog, I've got Harry Bosco on the phone and—" she saw the two strange men standing in her kitchen. Her eyes went wide with terror, then they squinted to glare at her husband. "Roger! What are you doing?!" She was as mad as a wet hen.

Doug smirked. His mom and dad talked to each other like that.

John put up his hands like he was in a holdup. He thought he saw a brief flash of gratitude flicker across Roger's face. There was an awkward silence for a few seconds before John broke it by saying, "We're sorry to disturb you, ma'am. There's an emergency."

Roger looked deep into John's eyes and said "Give me the phone, Dottie." He reached behind him with his left hand while keeping the gun trained on the two strangers in his kitchen. "And put on some coffee."

She stood about five feet behind him, glaring. He couldn't see her, but he could feel her eyes on his back. "Please," he said, a little bit louder.

That broke her trance. Roger didn't say "please" very often. She handed him the phone and scuttled over to the stove.

Just like my mom, thought Doug.

"Harry? Roger Kendrick. Yeah, we're shoveled out. Listen, I got two boys here—I think they're skiers—," he looked at John who smiled and nodded a confirmation. Roger was ignoring the other man on purpose. That guy reminded him of his cousin Jimmy.

"No, not that kind of skiers," Roger continued, "The ones that ski on flat ground."

"Cross country," Doug said, under his breath.

Roger gave Doug a darting glare that told him that John was to do the talking.

"Yeah, Harry. Anyway, they claim that there's a car buried in the snow with a sick woman in it."

There was a pause while the sheriff responded.

"Yeah, I know about the couple they found dead in their car in the ditch out by Prinsburg," Roger continued, "terrible thing." There was a long silence as he waited for the next response.

Then Roger resumed the conversation. "Well that's just it," his voice slowed down and took on a deeper tone, "they claim the car's buried along the Luce Line." He looked over at Doug and John. They'd better be telling the truth. "No, not by a road," Roger continued, "they said it's two miles west of here." Roger thought about how strange this must sound. Now he wished that he had had a couple more minutes to talk to these boys before Dottie got the sheriff on the line.

After the sheriff responded, Roger diverted his conversation to John. "Which side of the grade?"

John had since put his hands down. He responded by pointing to the north.

"Yeah, Harry. The north side, by the grove of pines at the back of the Schmidt farm."

Sheriff Harry Bosco had been listening to Roger with very tired ears.

He let out a deep sigh. *"You're not puttin' me on, are ya, Rog?"*

Harry and Roger had some history. They had gone to the same high school. There were practical jokes—and girls—involved, and Roger had gotten some laughs at Harry's expense. It was a long time ago, but some things you never forget.

Roger listened to silence on the line. This time it lasted at least ten seconds.

"It's been a long coupla days, Rog," Harry's voice was deep and firm.

Roger had been scrutinizing the two skiers. The one with the sweater, looked sincere. The other guy had a devilish smirk on his face. *That one can piss up a rope,* he thought. "I got 'em here standing in Dottie's kitchen," Roger said, to break the silence.

After a few seconds, he added, "the Ruger's on 'em." That ought to get Harry's attention.

Harry leaned back in his car seat. "*Is Roger crazy? Dottie's gonna kill him.*" Harry had dated Dottie briefly in high school. She was a handful then. She still was.

"*Well, I ain't gonna walk through two miles of snowdrifts tonight,*" Harry sighed. "*Can you get Barney to plow the grade? He can get on at Roseland. Tell him to push right through to "71."*" Harry tapped his fingers on his car phone for a few seconds, as he thought about the situation. "*Oh, yeah—and remind him to use the single-axle truck. The grade out there is pretty narrow.*"

"Okay, Harry, I'll call him," Roger replied.

"*Tell Barney I'll meet him in Roseland in half an hour.*" Harry hung up.

"Dottie," Roger said, handing the cordless phone to her, "get a hold of Barney."

"Oh, honey," Dottie replied, "he's got to be dead tired." She looked genuinely concerned. Plowing snow was one of the many jobs that her brother Barney did as an employee of Kandiyohi County.

"Do it," Roger said firmly. "Harry needs the Luce Line plowed from Roseland to the highway."

Doug and John looked at each other and smiled. They were making progress.

Barney picked up the phone on the first ring. He was so tired that he couldn't fall asleep, so he was on his couch watching an old "M*A*S*H" rerun.

He didn't have a clue as to what was happening on TV, but it was better than lying in bed watching the ceiling fan swirl around. He'd been awake for sixty-two hours straight. A new personal record.

It was his oldest sister on the line.

"Barney? Are you okay?" Dottie asked him anxiously.

"*Yeah.*" He was slow to reply. "*What's up, sis?*"

Dottie thought Barney sounded scary, like he was a zombie or something. She didn't want to talk to him when he sounded like that. "Here," she said, handing the phone to her husband. "You talk to him."

Roger took the phone from her. "Barney!" he said, loud and firmly, the way an older man talks when addressing his wife's little brother. Roger was only twelve years older than Barney, but forty years ago—when Roger married Dottie—that age difference was huge. Old family dynamics are like old dogs, they never change, they just get more bizarre with the passage of time.

"The sheriff needs the Luce Line plowed from Roseland to Blomkest."

Barney started laughing, very loud. "*Sure he does, Rog!*" His laugh became higher pitched.

"Barney!" Roger yelled again "Listen! I'm serious. He's going to meet you in Roseland in half an hour."

Barney stopped laughing. "*This isn't one of your jokes, is it, Rog?*" There was pain in his voice.

As the youngest boy in the family, he had been the brunt of many pranks.

"*You know, Rog,*" Barney said softly, "*I like a good joke as much as anyone.*" It was true. Barney was the most good-natured man that Roger had ever met. "*But I'm so tired,*" Barney mumbled, "*that I don't know if I'm on foot or horseback.*"

Roger lowered his voice, "It's not a joke. If you're too tired, I'll come and get the keys."

Roger heard him swear. He knew Barney wouldn't let anyone drive one of "his" trucks.

"*No, Rog,*" Barney said, tiredly. "*I'll meet Harry in Roseland.*"

Roger began to hang up the phone, when he remembered to tell him something else.

"Wait, Barney! You need to use the single-axle plow truck."

"*Yeah, I know,*" Barney replied, putting on his coveralls, "*the old railroad grade's narrow.*"

That made Roger feel better. At least Barney was awake enough to think.

"And wing it all to the south," Roger recalled. John gave Roger a "thumbs up."

"*Why?*" asked Barney.

"Harry will tell you." Roger paused for a moment, then added "Thanks, Barney."

"*Sure,*" Barney responded in surprise. Roger never said "thank you." Not to anyone. *It must be pretty serious*, Barney thought as he hung up the phone.

John had been watching Roger intensely during the entire conversation.

Doug had been looking at a batch of cupcakes on the counter next to the stove. *They must be homemade,* he thought, *they're still in the pan.*

Roger looked at the two strangers standing in his kitchen.

"You boys had better be telling the truth," he said sharply.

John looked down at the gun for a few seconds, then slowly raised his head and looked squarely into the eyes of his captor. "Why would we lie?" he responded.

Roger let out a heavy sigh.

Meanwhile, Doug couldn't take his eyes off those cupcakes.

"You're not really going to shoot us, are you, Roger?" John's query was tired, but firm.

Roger looked over his shoulder at his wife. She had her back to him, keeping busy with a washcloth, pretending to clean the stove.

It wasn't dirty.

While still holding it at his hip, Roger raised the barrel of the gun and pointed it at John for a couple of seconds, then pulled it up and pointed it at the ceiling. He walked over to the refrigerator and leaned his rifle up against the wall, then motioned for Doug and John to sit down next to him, at the kitchen table.

"Dottie," he said quietly, "get these boys some coffee."

CHAPTER 10

⎯⟋⟍✹⟋⟍⎯

Bob was looking down at a vision from his distant past.

His mind quickly grasped reality. It couldn't be his sister. She was dead. She was thirty-two when she passed away. He was with her when she died, and that was over twelve years ago. He had even shoveled dirt onto her casket.

Even so, now it looked like she was lying there right in front of him, as a child.

"My God," he said in a hoarse whisper, "she looks just like the way I remember her."

"What! Whad'ja say?" Bernie turned around to look in the back of the van.

"There's a little girl back here," Bob said louder.

"Wendy," the woman muttered.

Bob looked down at the pretty pale face of the little girl. Her eyes were closed.

She looks so peaceful, he thought, *just like my sister looked, after she passed on.*

A different type of horror struck him. He gasped – *"Oh no, she's gone too! We're too late!"* The agonizing thought brought a lump to his throat. He gently brushed her cheek with the back of his right hand. The loss of his sister came flooding back again. The grief squeezed the air out of his lungs, and he started to pass out.

Then, in the gray shadows of the minivan encased in snow, he thought he saw a soft flash of light flicker across her face. Brilliant blue eyes opened to greet him. The little girl's smile took a piece of his heart.

It had been over an hour since Doug and John had skied into the blackness to find help in Blomkest. Bernie had total confidence that Doug would find somebody that could alert the authorities about the situation, but he also knew that without John there, Doug could just as easily wind up in jail for throwing a rock through a window, or setting off car alarms.

So, together, Doug and John made a great team. Perseverance and brains.

Bernie did his best at watching over the woman by telling her dry Finnish jokes, and singing Marshal Tucker tunes. "Keep sick people awake and alert until the doctor comes," his mom had always told him. Bernie wished that his mom was here to help. She'd know exactly what to do.

All the sick woman could do, was manage an occasional weak smile, and drink a little Scotch and water. She was much calmer now that the little girl had been found. She often tried to speak, but "Wendy" was all that came out.

Bob was in the back of the van, just looking at the little girl's face. Her eyes would open for a while, then close again, as if she was going in and out of sleep. Bob wanted to give her some water, but was afraid to with the liquor in it.

For the first time that he could remember, Bob was ashamed of his drinking problem. He had talked to Bernie about going back to their campsite to get some fresh water, but neither one of them wanted to leave the person he was attending to.

Every minute that they waited for help to arrive, was agonizing to Bob. He knew that he had drunk a little too much when he was younger, but it never kept him from training or competing. When he got older, he used alcohol as a reward for getting through the day. Now, at forty, his day began with a drink, ran on a few "bumps" during the day, and ended with a nightcap–or two—or three. Not enough to be debilitating, but certainly enough to keep him from reaching his full potential.

Or help out a little girl in need.

Bob remembered when he started drinking. He was fourteen. That summer he had split off from his friends, Doug and John, and hung out with a different group of guys. They were more exciting—hanging out with wilder girls, stealing bicycles at the beginning of the summer and graduating to cars by the fall, shaking down younger kids for their money, and just plain being bad-asses. It was fun for a young man who had gotten used to getting picked on most of his life. A little payback.

The older brother of one of the boys got a kick out of supplying the boys with liquor. This opened up a whole new world for Bob. Most significantly, it gave him the opportunity to rebel openly against his father. It made him feel like he had one up on his dad.

By Thanksgiving of that year, all of the other delinquents had been rounded up and sent to Lino Lakes Reform School for penance and some attitude adjustment. All except Bob. Somehow he had come away clean—except for his alcohol addiction. Right after his sister died, his addiction increased considerably. Everyone saw it except his parents. They spent most of their thoughts grieving over the loss of their daughter. She had been the jewel of the family. Every year since her death, Bob's drinking problem had gotten a little worse.

Bob looked up at the back of Bernie's head in the passenger seat in front of him.

"Bern," Bob said loudly, trying to get his attention. Bernie was still sitting in the passenger seat, now singing an off-key version of The Marshall Tucker Band's "Hiding In The Desert Sky."

"Yeah what?" Bernie stopped singing and glanced back at him.

"I lied," Bob said sadly. "The demo bid could have waited until we got back. I didn't drive with you guys so I could drink in the car." Bob looked down and shook his head.

Bernie turned to face Bob, then smiled at him sadly. "I know, pal. It's alright."

Even though they had been great friends for many years, Bob saw Bernie in a different light after that. The words "like a brother," just weren't enough anymore.

A few minutes later, Bernie heard a low-pitched roaring sound coming down the railroad grade, from the west. He got out of the minivan to take a look.

A single-axle dump truck with a big plow was coming at them at about twenty miles per hour.

A car with flashing lights on its roof was about a quarter of a mile behind it.

Neither vehicle was using a siren.

Bob couldn't hear them from the back seat of the minivan, but he could feel the vibration of the truck plow as it got closer. He yelled out to Bernie, "Is help finally here?'"

Bernie looked back into the van with a puzzled look on his face. "I think so, but I'm not sure."

"What? What do you mean?"

It wasn't exactly what Bernie expected. *The snow-plow makes sense,* he thought, *but where is the ambulance? Even out here, they must have paramedics. What is the car for?*

The truck plow was coming up fast, winging the snow to the south, off the old railroad grade. When it got alongside Bernie, the vehicle stopped. The driver side window was open, and Bernie could hear a familiar song by George Strait blasting from the radio inside.

A large man, a little older than Bernie and Bob, leaned out of the window of the plow truck. He sounded very tired and haggard. "Whatcha got goin' on here?" he asked Bernie suspiciously.

Bernie was about to answer him, when the large man said, "You might be in trouble, son." A bright light struck Bernie in the face, blinding him. He winced at the pain in his eyes. The light came from the car behind the plow truck.

There was a brief blast of a siren as the car approached the back of the plow truck.

The truck driver gave Bernie one wave of his left hand and resumed plowing east down the grade. Sparks flew from the bottom of his plow as the metal hit the gravel.

The car with the flashing lights stopped a little short of where Bernie was standing. Its' spotlight was still shining on him. Bernie couldn't see it because of the bright light in his eyes, but the name on the side of the car read "Kandiyohi County Sheriff." The car sat there idling for well over a minute. Bernie shielded his eyes from the blinding spotlight.

Where's the ambulance? Bernie thought again. *And what did that plow driver mean?*

Finally, the car door opened and a thin man in khaki clothing slowly got out.

He was about sixty years old. He had his service revolver drawn and pointing at Bernie.

"Turn around and put your hands on top of the door," the sheriff said firmly.

Bernie was flabbergasted. "What?!" he yelled back. He had never had a gun pointed at him before. Not in his entire life. On occasion, Bernie and his friends indulged themselves in a paint ball game, but that didn't count. Those weren't *real* guns.

"You heard me. Do it now." The Sheriff sounded serious.

Bernie turned around slowly and did what he was told, dazed.

Bob heard the banter going on outside the van and quietly sat down next to Wendy.

"So what's going on here, boy?"

Bernie wanted to poke the officer in the eye with his ski pole. He was fuming mad. Instead, he answered shakily, "There's a sick woman in the van. She needs help."

"The hell you say." He didn't sound convinced.

"Really. If you don't believe me, come take a look for yourself," Bernie said, a little less rattled.

"You're not messing with me, are you, son?"

Bernie was outraged at the accusation. He spun around to face the officer.

"Goddammit!" he screamed. "Why the hell would I do that?"

The reality of his action struck him immediately. *Was that a leap of faith, or just plain stupidity?*

Sheriff Bosco was startled at the bold move made by the man standing below him.

"Thank God his hands are still in the air," he almost blurted out loud. The sheriff's exhausted mind analyzed the situation as quickly as it could.

The spotlight on his cruiser illuminated a confusing scene in front of him.

That was no kid standing down there. A backpack was lying in the snow, as was a thin glove and two ski poles, but no skis. The man holding his hands in the air, appeared to be sober. The vehicle the man was standing next to, was completely covered by snow except for a small patch of roof and an area around the passenger-side front door. The snow wasn't disturbed anywhere else.

The spotlight from the sheriff's car, cast shadows across the snow drifts behind the vehicle buried in the snow. The scenario would make sense if it was along the highway or even a side road, but not here, along the old railroad grade.

This wasn't what the sheriff expected to find on this long winter's night, out here on the prairie.

He expected to find nothing.

Sheriff Bosco had been plagued for several years by pranks perpetrated by three brothers from around Litchfield. He had never caught any of them in the act, but he was pretty sure that they were the ones keeping him and his deputy on their toes. He had arrested their cousin in a drug bust in 1991. That kid was still in jail, and would be for a few more years. The whole lot of them were bad news, but fairly smart. They never did anything violent, just really disruptive.

Sending a sheriff and a plow truck out on the Luce Line trail in the middle of a cold night after a big storm would be right up their alley. It would be a big joke. You could get a lot of drinks bought for you at the bar with a story like that. Sheriff Bosco didn't want to be regarded as a fool, but—as an officer of the law and a public servant—he was obligated to check out any story involving a hurt or stranded motorist. Even if it was called in by his old rival, Roger Kendrick.

The sheriff let out a deep breath. He was tired and irritable. The last few days had been long and hard. The storm had wreaked havoc with the power and the telephone lines, and it had cut Willmar (and every other town around there) off from the rest of the world for several days.

And now the sheriff had to deal with this. Two guys, who were skiing after midnight, in the fields, claim they found a car buried in the snow along the old railroad grade, with a sick woman in it. The car had to have been there for at least three days.

None of it made sense.

But there was a car, down in the ditch. And there was a man, about forty, *wearing knickers*, standing next to it with his arms in the air. And he looked furious.

The drunken brothers were clever, but this seemed out of their league. Two guys waking up and fooling Roger Kendrick in the middle of the night? It was possible, but not likely. Planting a car, on the Schmidt farm, before the storm? That was too elaborate for the brothers.

Sheriff Bosco really wanted to get those pranksters, but this didn't fit. He put his gun back into the holster. There could still be danger lurking in the van, but he didn't think so.

He reached into his car and got his jacket, gloves, and hat and put them on.

"I'm coming down there," he yelled to the man standing next to the van.

Bernie still had his arms up in the air. He painted houses for a living. He could hold them up all day if he had to. He was still thinking about how foolish he just was. *Spinning around and swearing at a cop pointing a gun at me? Am I insane?!*

Sheriff Bosco's eyes were on Bernie as the officer made his way down the embankment through the deep snow. The sheriff slid up alongside Bernie and looked into the van.

"Mary, Mother of God," sheriff Bosco said softly. The sheriff looked over at Bernie with tired eyes and said, "I guess I should call the ambulance."

Bernie gave him a cold stare. "We thought you *were* the ambulance."

Sheriff Bosco started up the embankment. "No," he said, "I thought it was a prank." He looked over his shoulder and gave Bernie a weak smile. "You did good. You can put your arms down now." Bernie slowly lowered his arms while glaring at the sheriff. Bernie's heart was still in his throat.

"A prank?" he yelled at the sheriff. "Really?!"

The sheriff trudged up the embankment and turned around to look at Bernie. "Don't worry, son," he said softly, "I told them to be at the ready. They're just waiting on my call." There was a hint of apology in his voice as he climbed into his idling car and got on the two-way radio.

Bernie was still shaking all over, and not from the cold.

In the back of the van, Bob was talking softly to the little girl. "Help will be here soon, Wendy." He liked the name "Wendy." It seemed to fit the little girl perfectly.

Bernie was starting to calm down. He climbed into the van and sat down, leaving the door open.

The sheriff rolled his car window down. "How you doin', son? Do you need to warm up?"

Sheriff Bosco knew that he couldn't move the woman, and she looked warm with a thick quilt around her, but the bearded man wearing knickers didn't have to stay out in the cold.

Bernie looked up at the sheriff and yelled, "No, I'm okay. I better stay and keep her company."

Sheriff Bosco rolled up his window and smiled. *He seems like a nice guy,* he thought, *that woman is really lucky he found her. But how in the devil did all this come about?*

"I'll talk to him after the ambulance comes," he muttered, "I'll get a full report then."

The sheriff still had no idea that there were two more people in the minivan. In his tired state, he hadn't looked inside, and—in all the commotion— Bernie thought he had told him.

Less than ten minutes passed before Bernie heard the siren. It took a few more minutes before it shut off as the ambulance turned on to the Luce Line Trail. Harry had sent Barney in the plow truck back there to wait for it. As soon as the paramedics turned on to the trail, Barney high-tailed it for home. He was dreaming before his head hit the pillow on the couch. He had gone more than sixty-four hours without sleep. He never came close to breaking that record, even though he plowed snow for twenty more years.

"The cavalry's comin'," Bernie said to the sick woman. She seemed much more relaxed now. Most of Bob's water bottle was empty. Maybe it was a good thing there was Scotch in that bottle, but Bernie was surprised that she didn't throw up again.

Bob was still talking to the little girl. "Don't worry Wendy, I won't leave you."

He had repeated her name many times. He never got tired of saying it.

The step-van ambulance driven by the paramedic's pulled up behind the sheriff's car. It was from a hospital in Willmar.

The dark forms of a man and a woman jumped out, wearing warm jackets, gloves, hats and Sorel boots. They were well prepared for the subzero weather. The woman got a collapsible stretcher and a blanket from the back of the step-van, and both paramedics bounded down the embankment. Bernie did his best to get out of the way as the male paramedic brushed past him. "Thanks, but we'll take it from here," the young female paramedic said to Bernie, with a smile.

The male paramedic climbed into the passenger seat of the minivan, slowly reclined the driver's seat with the sick woman in it, and pulled up the armrest. He carefully wrestled her out of the seat while asking her, "Where does it hurt, ma'am? Is anything broken?"

Then he took a deep whiff of the sick woman's breath and asked her, "Have you been drinking?"

Bernie backed up behind the door of the minivan. He had Bob's water bottle in his right hand.

He slid it deep into the snow beside him.

The male paramedic emerged from the minivan holding the limp figure of the sick woman in his arms. She looked to be about thirty years old, with long, sandy-colored hair and a thin build.

Bernie gazed at the sick woman and thought, *that's funny. I never really noticed anything about her before, except that she was sick. She's really quite pretty.*

Bernie helped the female paramedic open the collapsible stretcher. The male paramedic gently laid the sick woman on the stretcher, looked at her face, and smiled as he said, "You sure are a mess, aren't you? But don't worry, we'll clean you up and take good care of you." He tucked the hospital blanket tightly around her. She gave him a weak smile in response to his kind words.

Bernie noticed that the eyes of the sick woman had gotten duller after the paramedics arrived, and she looked more at peace than he had seen her since he and Bob had found her. Bernie thought he knew that look, and he didn't like it.

Now that she knew her little girl was going to be safe, the sick woman was letting go.

The male paramedic went to relieve Bernie of the stretcher handles that were in his hands.

"I got it covered, chief," Bernie said to him in a solemn tone.

The paramedic looked into Bernie's eyes. Those eyes told him that he would have to fight Bernie to get the handles. The male paramedic looked over at the female paramedic and said softly, "Kathy, could you go and open the doors on the truck? We've got it covered here."

Kathy flashed a quick smile of gratitude at Bernie as she handed her stretcher handles over to her partner, then scrambled up the embankment to wait for them.

Bernie and the paramedic carried the sick woman up to the railroad grade. They slipped a few times, but the stretcher never touched the snow.

Kathy pulled a full-size gurney out of the back of the van and set the wheels on the snow-packed grade. The two men laid the stretcher on the gurney and lifted it into the back of the truck. The male paramedic hopped in next to the gurney and immediately started checking the vital signs of the sick woman as Kathy closed the doors behind him. Kathy turned to Bernie with a warm smile that seemed to contain more than gratitude and said, "Thank you." Kathy hitched her thumb in the direction of the truck. "She's very lucky you found her."

Bernie really looked at the face of the female paramedic for the first time. He saw hope, sadness, family, comfort and even love in her eyes. He was drawn to her so strongly that he backed up a step and took a deep breath. He had never experienced feelings this intense before.

"I didn't find her," he said softly. He felt like he was giving a confession in church.

"You didn't?" Kathy said quietly, giving him a puzzled look. "Then who did?"

When Bernie and the male paramedic were putting the woman on the gurney, Bob was sliding his sore left hand under Wendy's legs. The pain in his hand from the knife cut only throbbed a little now. He put his right arm behind her back, and lifted her off the bench seat while still on his knees. *She's so frail,* he thought, *so slight.*

Wendy put her arms around his neck and squeezed tight. "Thank you," a tiny voice whispered in his ear. Tears blurred his vision as he slowly spun her around.

"Can you walk?" he asked her.

"Unh-uh," she whispered in response.

A revelation washed over him. The wheelchair was hers.

For a second, the strength in Bob's arms gave out and he almost dropped her, then he caught his breath and set Wendy on the front passenger seat and crawled over her to get out of the minivan.

The spotlight on the sheriff's car had been providing more than enough light for the rescue operation. At the brightest point, by the door of the minivan, the snow looked like dirty diamonds. Along the peripheral edges, in the snowdrifts beyond the van, the light cast shadows that were so eerie they even made the paramedics shudder. The spotlight overpowered all of the other light around it, making it look like this bizarre scene was the only place left on earth.

From the top of the grade, the door of the minivan, surrounded by snow, seemed to be an entrance into the underworld. Bernie responded to the female paramedic by pointing at the black abyss. "He found her."

A short, stocky man emerged from the hole in the snow. The small, thin body of a child was in his arms. Bob closed his eyes and turned his face away from the light.

Kathy took a step forward and looked over at Bernie. "Are there any others?" she asked.

Bernie looked back at Kathy with surrender in his eyes. "No," he said softly.

Kathy took another step toward the minivan buried in the snow. She was going to help Bob. Bernie reached down and took hold of Kathy's hand. She looked over at him again. Bernie shook his head "no."

Bob was struggling up the embankment, carrying the little girl.

"That's my friend, Bob," Bernie said to Kathy. She looked at Bernie, smiled and squeezed his hand hard before letting it go.

Kathy walked to the back of the ambulance and opened the door, "Curt," she said, "We have another one,...."

"What!?" the male paramedic responded, startled at the news. He looked over his shoulder at her.

" ....a little girl," Kathy finished.

Curt got up and shuffled his way to the back of the ambulance. "We've got to go soon," he said to Kathy. "She's really sick. Some kind of flu virus, and I think she has pneumonia. Her temp's 103.8. We've got to get her to the hospital. *Now.*"

Curt looked past Kathy. Bob was standing there, patiently holding the little girl in his arms. Kathy scrambled to get out of his way. Bob walked up to the open door.

"Be careful," he said. "She can't walk."

Wendy didn't want to let go. Her arms tightened around his neck.

Curt laid several blankets on the floor, next to the gurney.

"I want to go with them," Bob said firmly.

Kathy looked over at Bob with a sad look on her face. "There's no room. We didn't know there would be more than one, or we would've taken the bigger truck," she said apologetically.

Curt looked at them both. "The bigger truck wouldn't fit down this narrow old railroad grade."

Sheriff Bosco had been catnapping in his warm cruiser. No one could blame him for that. He hadn't seen Bob come out of the minivan. He woke up and looked down at the vehicle buried in the snow. The bearded man that he had thought might be a prankster, was standing down there alone. It looked like Curt and Kathy were done. He put on his gloves and his Stetson hat, got out of his car, and walked to the back of the ambulance. He saw Bob holding the little girl.

"Who the hell are you?" he asked Bob, startled. He was shocked by the latest development. "And where did she come from?" The sheriff knew it was a dumb question when he asked it.

"She was in the minivan, too," Kathy answered, pointing at Wendy. Then she raised her finger and pointed at Bob. "He found them."

"But the other guy never said anything about her," the sheriff said, glaring down at Bernie. Then he remembered how they met. *Under the circumstances, I probably wouldn't have said anything either*, he thought. He wasn't so much surprised at the newcomers, as he was embarrassed. He should have checked out the minivan himself. He quickly changed the subject.

"So what's the verdict?" the sheriff asked, turning back to look at Curt.

"We've got to go," the paramedic responded. "This woman is really sick."

Kathy was pulling Wendy's arms away from Bob's neck as gently as she could.

"It's okay, honey," Kathy said softly to her, "we're going to take you with your mommy."

149

"Can't daddy come, too?" Wendy asked, in a small frail voice.

The eyes of Curt, Kathy, and the sheriff tracked over to Bob. Kathy cocked her head to the side and looked at Bob inquisitively.

With dull eyes, Bob returned their stares and shook his head "no." Bob looked down at the little girl in his arms and said softly, "It's all right, sweetheart. You go with mommy. I'll see you soon."

Bob reluctantly released the little girl to Kathy, and Curt helped place Wendy on the blankets next to her mother.

Bob fell to his knees when Curt closed the door to the ambulance.

"Hold on there, buckaroo," Sheriff Bosco's firm hand grabbed Bob's shoulder before he fell face first in the snow. "Hey!" the sheriff yelled down to Bernie. "Is your buddy okay?"

Bernie had been gathering up Bob's stuff down by the minivan. He had gotten his glove, hatchet and flashlight and zipped them back into Bob's backpack. Bernie slipped the almost-empty Scotch and water bottle into his own jacket. Then he found the plastic bottle full of undiluted Scotch in Bob's backpack and slipped that into his own jacket as well. *I promised Linda that I would try to curb Bob's drinking,* he thought. Bernie was digging Bob's skis out of the snow when the sheriff called down to him. He looked up to respond, "What's that?"

"Is your buddy here sick?" the sheriff asked him.

"I don't think so," Bernie yelled back. "He's probably just exhausted." He pondered for a moment and added, "and really out of shape." Bernie looked at Bob for a reaction.

When he didn't get a sarcastic retort, he thought, *Maybe he is sick.*

Bernie threw Bob's backpack over his shoulder, grabbed his skis and poles and headed up the embankment. He was looking forward to a long snooze in his warm sleeping bag.

"Hey, fella," the sheriff said with a smile. He was looking down at the man he was propping up. "Why don't you come with me? I'd like to ask you some questions."

"I'm camping with my friends," Bob muttered in response. He pointed toward the grove of trees.

"Well," the sheriff responded, "I don't think you could make it that far. Besides, that's an illegal campsite." Bernie had gotten back up on the railroad grade. He looked sharply at the sheriff.

Sheriff Bosco caught Bernie's concerned look. The sheriff winked and shook his head "no."

Bernie caught the wink and smiled at the sheriff. "That's probably a pretty good idea, Bob," Bernie agreed. "I'll take care of your skis and poles. We can meet up tomorrow."

Bob's foggy mind thought, *Tomorrow? Would that be after this night is over? Or the morning of the day after that?* It seemed like a lifetime had passed since he had gotten out of that Cadillac near Gluek. His mind was reeling with a thousand thoughts.

"C'mon, son. I'll take you back to my house," the sheriff continued. "A good night's sleep and a hot meal will do you some good." He looked over at Bernie and smiled, "You want to come too?"

Bernie was still smiling at the sheriff, "No thanks, officer. Our tents are up and our other friends should be back soon. I'd better hang out here."

"Officer?" the sheriff said. "Hell, I'm Harry." The sheriff extended his hand for Bernie to shake.

Bernie shook Harry's hand in earnest. "I'm Bernie," he said, "and this is my friend Bob."

Harry extended his right hand to Bob, who was still on his knees.

Bob looked like "death warmed over," as Bob's dad used to say.

Even as exhausted as he was, Bob reached up and almost crushed the sheriff's hand.

"OUCH!" Harry yelled, yanking his hand away from Bob's powerful grip.

Harry looked over at Bernie, who had a smirk on his face. Bernie nodded in recognition. He knew Bob's crushing handshake all too well.

Harry smiled with a nervous laugh, while trying to shake the pain out of his hand.

The sheriff looked back at Bernie. "Sorry about the holdup," he said, apologetically.

Bernie had already put the incident out of his mind. It wasn't in him to hold a grudge.

"Oh, that?" Bernie laughed a little, too. "It's okay. You can never be too careful."

"Man, when you spun around . . .," Harry paused to sigh and shake his head.

"Yeah, I know," Bernie said sheepishly. "It could have gotten ugly. I'll have to clean out my shorts when I get back to camp." They both laughed louder.

"No hard feelings?" Harry asked.

"Not a chance," was Bernie's sincere response.

Kathy leaned out of the driver's side window of the ambulance and yelled, "Hey, Harry! We're ready to go!" Kathy gave Bernie a warm smile and waved to him.

Bernie waved back. He didn't want her to go. He felt like a lovesick teenager.

The sheriff's cruiser was parked in front of the ambulance. There was no way to get around it on the narrow grade.

Harry looked back at Bernie. "I'll bring him back tomorrow," he said, "you'll be here?"

"We'll be here," Bernie said firmly. Bernie handed Bob's old backpack over to Harry, then helped Bob stand up and walked him over to the sheriff's cruiser.

Bernie looked deep into Bob's eyes. "Tomorrow," he said solemnly.

Bob caught the stare and nodded. "Tomorrow."

"Not too early," Harry said, helping Bob into the front seat of his car. Bernie nodded.

It was a little after two o'clock in the morning when the sheriff's cruiser and the ambulance drove off in silence. Bernie watched until the taillights disappeared from view. When the vehicle's got to the highway, he saw their flashing lights come on and heard the sirens start up. It took several minutes before the sound was swallowed up by the night.

Bernie stood silently, listening, until he couldn't hear them anymore.

Bernie let out a heavy sigh, picking up Bob's skis and poles, and then it struck him.

Where was his stuff?!

He remembered that he had taken off his skis and poles when Bob had called for help in the ditch. Bernie looked around in the darkness. His eyes were still recovering from the glare of the spotlight. "I should have kept Linda's flashlight," he said out loud, recalling that he had zipped it into one of the pockets in Bob's old backpack.

He saw something shiny sticking out of the plowed snow windrow on the south side of the grade. It was one of his aluminum ski poles. He fished it out of the packed snow.

It was bent at a forty-five-degree angle. Bernie frowned and used the pole to dig for the other one. He found it unscathed. He smiled, but then his heart sank. *Where are my skis?*

He found his prized Peltonen skis lying on the north edge of the grade, parallel to the trail, just inches from the plow cut.

That's strange, he pondered, *I know that I took them off in the middle of the trail, so how did they get here?* He thought about it briefly, then shrugged it off.

Suddenly, his eyes caught movement in the western sky.

Two brilliant meteorites streamed across the heavens, from north to south.

"Wow," Bernie uttered in amazement, "look at that. Too bad Bob's not here to see it."

He and Bob had spent many hours gazing into the universe, watching the northern lights, counting the stars, and looking for strange objects. Bob told Bernie that he was especially fascinated by the sky, but he didn't know why. Over the years, the fascination had rubbed off on Bernie. He watched the burning objects as they vanished over the horizon.

Bernie snapped out of his trance, and looked down at his bent ski pole.

Oh well, he thought, *only one thing destroyed. Not bad considering a plow truck drove by.*

Standing alone on the desolate prairie in the star-studded blackness, Bernie mused over the events of this extraordinary night. *"Collateral damage,"* he laughed out loud.

He was thinking of his bent ski pole—and the gorgeous paramedic he had just met.

"Doug and John should be along soon," he muttered to himself as he snapped on his beloved skis and started single-poling his way down the unplowed edge of the grade toward their campsite. He had much to tell his friends.

As he skied up to his tent, Bernie started feeling guilty about taking Bob's booze.

"He'll need it in the morning," he said out loud, looking up, like he was asking for forgiveness. "I'll give it back to him then."

Bernie felt the confirmation of his resolution settle softly on his shoulders. It gave him peace, but he knew he wouldn't be doing Bob a favor.

He was too tired to wait up for his friends. The last of the campfire's glowing embers struggled for life as Bernie drifted off to sleep. His smiling mouth formed the name "Kathy" as a pleasant dream began to overtake his conscious thoughts.

Bernie and Kathy were married sixteen months later in a huge wedding in Willmar. It was his first— and would be his only time. Kathy was a widow with two young boys.

Bernie raised them as his sons.

His mother could not have been happier.

CHAPTER 11

—⌒⊱❈⊰⌒—

"Y ou boys are real heroes," Harry said to Bob. "If you hadn't come along, nobody would've found that minivan until spring."

Bob's head was leaning up against the window as he sat in the sheriff's cruiser. He was looking out across the snowy fields with sad, tired eyes. He didn't feel like a hero.

"How did you happen to come across that car, anyway?" Harry asked, looking over at Bob. He needed to know this for the report that he had to file, but he was just as interested in hearing the story to satisfy his own curiosity.

Just then, the two-way radio speaker under the car dashboard started blaring. It was the sheriff's office's night dispatcher. She worked from home. Harry's home. The night dispatcher was his wife.

"*Harry? Are you there?*" An anxious female voice came across the airwaves.

The sheriff picked up and keyed the two-way radio mic. "Yeah, Donna, I'm here," he answered.

"*So what's going on?*" she asked, excitedly. "*Was Dottie's call for real?*"

"Yes, honey, it was," Harry responded. He looked over at Bob and smiled. Bob didn't notice. The sheriff frowned and looked back at the radio. *She's supposed to be sleeping,* he thought.

Harry had only gotten about eight hours of sleep in the last few days, due to the blizzard. For Donna, it had been even less. She couldn't rest until she was sure that everybody in the county was safe after the storm. The thought made him smile as it added another wrinkle to his forehead. "Mother to the people," he muttered to himself. He gazed down at the microphone in his hand and shook his head proudly, "A sheriff's devoted wife."

Harry reflected on the circumstances leading up to the events of this night. He and his deputy, Brent, usually shared two ten-hour shifts per day. Harry had the 6:00 a.m. to 4.00 p.m. shift, and Brent took the 4:00 p.m. to 2:00 a.m. shift. They both were on call from 2:00 a.m. to 6:00 a.m. They revolved this through the weekends, and another part-time deputy filled in on their days off. The sheriff and his deputy were supposed to each have two weeks of paid vacation per year, but neither one of them had taken a formal vacation in well over a decade. They both liked to hunt and fish, but that was readily available right around their county. And they loved their jobs. Their wives didn't seem to mind that their husbands never felt the need to go anywhere exotic. There were a lot of things to do around Willmar.

The storm had thrown everybody's schedules topsy-turvy. It happened every once in a while. When you live in a land of unpredictable weather, you take it all in stride.

But Donna was supposed to be sleeping. Harry held the microphone in his lap, and thought back a couple of hours. He had been just about ready to hang it up for the night when he got the call from Dottie. After he talked to Roger, he radioed Donna to tell her that he'd be home in a little while and she shouldn't wait up. After nearly forty years of marriage, he knew she wouldn't go to bed without him, but he had to say it anyway.

She's had half as much sleep as I've had, he thought, *and now I'm bringing a stranger home.*

Harry looked over at his passenger. Bob didn't seem like a stranger. There was something familiar about him. He felt like somehow he already knew this man. Puzzled by the thought, Harry keyed the mic again. "Honey, call Dottie back and tell her those skiers did good. They found a woman and a little girl buried in the snow. They're both alive, but the woman is really sick. And leave a message for Brent. Tell him to drive out in the morning on the Luce Line Trail east of Roseland. It's all plowed out. He'll find a minivan on the Schmidt farm just past the stand of pine trees. Tell him to see what he can find out about who owns it and why it's out there."

Donna was at their kitchen table, feverishly writing all this down. She had taken shorthand in high school, not knowing then how handy it would become in the years to follow. She took a deep breath and shook her hand as her husband resumed giving her directives.

"And tell Brent to bring a tow truck out with him," Harry continued. "We'll want to haul that minivan back to the fire station in Blomkest."

Harry put the microphone back in his lap and looked at Bob. His voice got softer and deeper, "Oh, and, honey, make sure the extra bed is made," Harry smiled at the thought. "I'm bringing a friend home for the night." Harry continued the conversation with his wife, but Bob didn't hear it.

Bob's exhausted mind had spun back to an argument that he had had with his own wife, at Christmas, a couple of weeks before. She had been trying to get him to go to church again.

"It's bullshit!" he had yelled at her. "A scam for sentimental suckers! Church and prayers didn't save my sister, did they? Where was God then?!"

"God watches over us *spiritually*," she had pleaded, "*if* we let him in. What happens to our bodies is subject to the whims of the physical world. That's why bad things can happen to good people. You can't blame God for your sister's death."

His mind thick with liquor, Bob had been unable to think of a good retort, so he had just stormed out of the house, the argument over for the moment. It was an old dispute. Bob and his wife had some variation of it around every religious holiday, going back to their wedding day, neither one of them willing to bend on their convictions.

But, deep inside, Bob wanted to believe again. The pain of helplessly watching his sister die and the torment he witnessed in the eyes of her husband and his parents, wouldn't let him give in. And the Scotch he had turned to for comfort, instead fueled his stubbornness.

Bob let out a heavy sigh as the evening glow of Willmar grew on the horizon.

What if she's right? Bob's brain squirmed at the notion. *What have I got to lose?*

For the first time in over a dozen years, Bob began to pray. He begged God with every fiber of his being to save the little girl and her mother. The bittersweet tears of surrender burned Bob's cheeks as he fell asleep, his head banging softly against the window of the sheriff's cruiser.

"This sure is good coffee, Mrs. Kendrick," Doug said with a cheesy smile, still eyeing up the cupcakes on the kitchen counter.

Roger Kendrick gazed out the kitchen window with a disgusted look on his face. Nobody saw it. His mind wandered. *What was the name of that TV show with the two brother's in it? I think it was back in the fifties. The older brother had a friend who was a real weasel.* Roger glanced over at Doug, *"This guy reminds me of him."* Roger looked back out the window at the streetlight casting a soft glow upon the snow.

Dottie saw Doug looking at her fresh batch of cupcakes. She liked him. Doug reminded her of Roger's cousin, Jimmy. The other guy, wearing the sweater with the Swedish flag knitted into it, was okay, but he seemed to be too serious, too much like Roger. Dottie brought the tray of fresh bakery to the table. She was smiling at Doug.

"Would you boys like some cupcakes?"

Roger was deep in thought. He was still trying to remember the name of the weasel. *I can't think of it,* he frowned, *but he was a real wise-ass, suck-up kind of a guy.* He looked down and smiled into his coffee cup. *"But, somehow, everybody liked him."*

The telephone rang at about the same time as John, Doug, and the Kendrick's heard the sirens. Dottie went over to the wall, picked up the phone, and carried it into the adjacent room. The call was brief.

"That was Donna," Dottie said, walking back into the kitchen. "She said you boys did good. She said they pulled a woman and a little girl—"

"A little girl?" John interrupted. "We only knew about the woman!"

Doug was on his third cupcake.

". . . a little girl out of the car," Dottie resumed. "The woman is really sick. They're on their way to the hospital in Willmar." Dottie smiled, pleased that she could deliver the news.

Roger looked over at the two strangers in his kitchen and managed a friendly smile. Despite Dottie's good coffee, both of the skiers looked haggard. Roger found himself saying, "You fellas are welcome to spend the night."

Many years later, Doug and John stood next to Barney as pallbearers at Roger Kendrick's funeral. Of the two, Roger had secretly liked Doug the best, but he had always referred to the both of them as "'my varmints'."

CHAPTER 12

B ob grabbed his old backpack, as Harry helped him out of the cruiser. Bob was stiff after his short nap in the warm car. They had pulled into a cobblestone driveway alongside a large, beautiful, old brick house. A soothing yellow glow radiated out of the windows. The dark form of a thin woman in a peach-colored sweat suit was standing in the side doorway.

"Oh, Harry, that poor woman and her little girl," Donna said with tears in her eyes as her husband and his new-found friend walked up to the door.

"Wendy," Bob mumbled.

"What's that?" asked Harry. It was the first word Bob had spoken since they left Bernie on the railroad grade next to the minivan.

"Wendy," Bob said louder. "The little girl's name is Wendy."

"How do you know that?" Harry asked him.

"The sick woman kept saying it over and over—that's how we found her."

"And we're so glad you did," Donna said with a smile, patting Bob's arm. "To think of it, buried for three days in the snow. It must have been terrifying."

They went into the house. A large, warm, inviting, country kitchen greeted them. Bob hesitated to step on the old wooden floor. Despite spending an hour or so in the minivan and about twenty minutes in the sheriff's car, his knee-high socks were still caked in melting ice.

"Oh, you don't worry about that, honey," Donna assured him. "It's just a little snow."

Bob thought, *A little snow will make a puddle, but a lot of snow can drown you.*

Harry motioned for Bob to sit down in a high-backed spindle chair next to the kitchen table.

Bob plopped into it like a sack of potatoes being thrown on a shelf. With a loud grunt, he bent over and untied his old kangaroo-skin ski boots and took them off. It felt good to wriggle his toes again after ten and a half hours.

He looked down at his wool socks. Normally they would have cotton poplin "gators" covering them, but he forgot to put them on back at the convenience store in Cosmos.

The gator's would have kept ice from collecting on his socks. Ice which was now melting, leaving a lake on Donna's bird's eye maple floor. Bob peeled off his left glove, covered with dried blood, and started to take his socks off. Donna saw him wince.

"Is there something wrong with your hands?" She was genuinely concerned.

Bob turned his left hand palm up. It was the first time he'd seen it in full light. There was a gash at least two inches long from the edge of his palm at his wrist, running up towards his middle finger. It was right on top of the old fishing line scar. The skin all around it was stained red. The wound wasn't that severe, but it looked ugly.

"Oh my gosh!" Donna gasped. "Harry! Come and take a look at this!"

Harry leaned over to take a peek. He wasn't happy with what he saw.

Harry looked deep into Bob's dull eyes. "I should have taken you to the doctor," he said firmly.

"No!" Bob said fuzzily. "It's okay. Just need some mercurochrome."

"Mercurochrome?!" Harry chuckled, "I haven't seen any of that stuff in years."

"Alcohol then," Bob retorted. The warm air in the kitchen was making him drowsy, and his hand was beginning to throb. And speaking of alcohol, he could sure go for a nightcap.

Harry put his hand on Bob's shoulder. "Really, son. I should take you to the hospital."

Bob hadn't been near a hospital since the awful night that he spent with his sister.

Bob didn't like hospitals. To him, they were where people go to die. He waved his right hand at Harry.

The little finger in that hand was throbbing too.

"No! I'm just tired," Bob almost shouted, "I just need some sleep. Really, I'll be fine."

Harry looked over at his wife. "Donna, could you get us a bowl and some alcohol?"

Harry looked back at Bob and smiled. "You're a stubborn mule." He had seen the look of fear in Bob's eyes. "But that's okay," Harry whispered, "I don't like hospitals either."

Donna was warming up homemade caramel rolls in the oven. They had a microwave on the counter, but Donna insisted that that was only for thawing things out in a hurry. It got used a couple of times a year. Without turning to face them, she got into the conversation.

"Oh, you guys! What is it with men and doctors? You really can't be that wimpy," Donna said disgustedly. "If you only knew what women go through ....."

Harry and Bob looked at each other, both scared of receiving "the lecture" that they knew all too well. It usually ended up with "When was your last physical?" or, even worse, "I need to schedule you for a colonoscopy." All married men secretly know that this is a way for their wives to get back at them for . . . whatever.

Harry interrupted Donna before she got too far. "Honey, did you get that alcohol?"

Donna turned to face them, gave them a dirty look, and trotted out of the room. Both men started breathing again.

Harry waited until Donna was gone, then turned to Bob. "So how did you get the cut?" he asked.

Bob seemed startled by the question. His eyes had followed Donna as she left the room. He couldn't believe how much she reminded him of his own wife. Bob looked back at Harry.

"Huh?"

"How did you get the cut on your hand?" Harry repeated, slowly.

"Fishing line," Bob said in a fog.

"Fishing line?!" Harry grunted.

"No! no," Bob's foggy mind returned to the present. "It was my pocket knife. I was trying to cut through the frost around the door of the minivan. It doesn't have a locking blade."

He reached back and felt for it. For the first time since his eighth birthday, it wasn't in his back pocket. A mild wave of panic washed over him. It must have fallen into the snow. He'd have to go out and find it tomorrow. He knew Bernie would help him.

Donna came back with a bowl, alcohol, and some swabs. Bob tucked away his panic and looked up at Donna. "I want to take my socks off first," he said.

He began to peel off his frozen woolen socks. When the exposed skin hit the warm air, it began to burn. Bob's calves were as red as cooked lobster, except for a few quarter-size white spots.

"You've got some frostbite there," Harry said, pointing at Bob's legs.

Bob looked at it. It wasn't too bad. "It's okay," he shrugged, "I've had it before."

Donna took Bob's hand and placed it in the bowl. She carefully dabbed his cut with Q-tips dipped in alcohol.

Bob knew the cut was deep. "Just pour it on," he said.

Donna looked at him and backed up. "Are you sure?" she asked, surprised.

"Yeah, I'm sure." Before she could do it, Bob picked up the bottle and poured it on his hand. He almost passed out as the pain shot up his arm like a hot dagger.

Harry had gotten a big aluminum pot out of a cupboard. He filled it with luke-warm water.

"Here, Bob. Put your legs in this. For the frostbite." Harry set the pot by Bob's feet.

Bob's head was swimming back to reality after the alcohol jolt, so he stood up, stepped into the pot, and sat back down. The warm water stung his legs at first, but soon felt soothing. He had done this many times in the past.

"When was your last tetanus shot?" Harry asked him, looking down at his hand.

Bob's mind was clearer now. "Five—no—four and a half years ago," he answered. "It was in a mobile clinic on a large construction site. Everyone on the job was required to be up to date."

"You should be good then," Harry said.

The caramel rolls were done. Along with real butter and hot cocoa, Bob felt the late-night snack was as good a meal as he ever had. He didn't even miss his nightcap.

Harry and Donna kept the conversation light. They asked Bob where he was from, what he did for a living, how he happened to be skiing the Luce Line Trail, and how long had he known his friends. Harry told Bob and Donna how he met Bernie. Donna thought it was awful that he almost shot Bernie, but Bob almost fell off his chair from laughing so hard.

Harry didn't ask Bob how he happened to find the minivan, even though he was dying to know. That would be official business and could wait until later.

As the stories were winding down, Bob's legs had returned to the right color, and Donna had bandaged his hand.

It's an excellent dressing, Bob thought, *as good as Bernie's mom could do it.*

Bob grabbed his backpack and followed Harry up the stairs to the guest room after getting a big hug from Donna. Bob noticed that there were antiques everywhere.

"The house has been in Donna's family for five generations," Harry said proudly.

Bob didn't think that he had ever crawled into a more comfortable bed.

It was 3:20 a.m.

Bob couldn't move his legs.

He could see his sister in the "56 Ford convertible through the passenger door window. The top was up on the car. His sister was frightened and screaming, but he couldn't hear her. Bob pawed at the snow, but the harder he dug, the deeper it got.

The snow was drifting up on the door. Bob was crawling to it, but the door stayed out of his reach. He looked over his shoulder, above him. Uncle Art was *standing* in the big green boat, holding a huge fishing rod. A pearl-handled pocket knife was bait. Uncle Art cast at the car just as the snowdrift covered the window. A massive hook caught the back bumper of the car and yanked it out of the snow. The bottom of the car was brilliant orange and gold. The pearl-handled pocket knife had come loose from the hook. The old car swallowed it and smiled, then disappeared into the amber liquid that the snow had become. Bob looked up. The big green boat was above him now. A dozen feet of Scotch separated him from the boat. A trap door was at the bottom of the boat. Bob reached for it, but it was rapidly floating away from him. Bob tried to swim, but he was drowning in the intoxicating liquid. He couldn't move his legs.

Bob sat up abruptly—awake and covered in a cold sweat.

He was momentarily disorientated.

A faint light was coming through a paned window graced with sheer taffeta curtains. Bob was in a large four-poster bed. A big bureau with an ornate mirror above it was across from him. The hands of the Sessions clock on the bureau read seven thirty. The house was quiet except for the faint ticking of the clock.

Bob fell back to sleep the moment his head touched the pillow.

It felt like only a moment later, that Harry was shaking Bob's shoulder.

"Ma's gettin' breakfast on," Harry said. "If you want to take a shower, there's fresh towels in the bathroom, down the hall and to the left."

"Thanks," Bob smiled, "a shower will feel good." He felt a hundred per cent better than he had the night before. He looked at the antique clock on the bureau. It was 10:45.

All the clothes he was wearing last night— knickers, wool socks, and all—had been washed and neatly folded and were lying on an ancient captain's chair in his room.

"When does she sleep?" he said to himself in awe of Donna who obviously had done this unsolicited but much appreciated task. Bob smiled and began humming "Up on Cripple Creek." Once again, Donna reminded him of the amazing angel in his own life.

Bob bounced down the stairs feeling clean and refreshed, like a new man. The smell of bacon and pancakes filled his senses and he realized that he was ravenously hungry. On his way down the stairs, he noticed three graduation pictures on the wall — two boys and a girl. Judging by the hair-styles, they weren't much younger than him. Harry was reading the newspaper at the kitchen table. He looked up.

"Sleep well, son?" Harry said with a smile.

"Better than I have since I don't know when," Bob said, returning his smile.

Bob and Harry sat down to a phenomenal breakfast of fresh fruit, homemade muffins, scrambled eggs, blueberry pancakes, maple bacon, orange juice, whole milk, and the best coffee Bob ever had in his life. It looked like Donna was expecting an army.

Bob thought that he knew why. "So do your kids live around here?" Bob asked his hosts.

Harry responded, "Brian, our oldest, is a lieutenant colonel in the Air Force, stationed in Germany right now. Cheryl is a vet. Moved to Seattle with her husband two years ago. Danny is an electrical engineer. Works for Honeywell in the Twin Cities. He lives in St. Louis Park."

Harry said this all matter-of-factly, without putting down his newspaper. Donna was at the stove, with her back to the men. She sighed and said sadly, "We never see them anymore."

Bob did his best to eat all the food Donna had prepared with her children in mind.

After breakfast, Donna took a look at Bob's hand. "It looks like it's coming along okay," she said, "the color is back and the swelling is down." She put a new dressing on his wound.

Donna kissed her husband on the cheek and gave Bob a big hug as he and Harry went out the door. Bob gave her a big hug back, thanking her for their tremendous hospitality.

"You change that dressing at least once a day," she said. "And don't be a stranger."

Bob smiled and waved to her. It suddenly occurred to him how much he missed his own parents. Bob tossed his backpack into the backseat of the sheriff's cruiser, and got into the passenger seat.

It was a beautiful morning—almost afternoon. Milder air had moved in. The temperature had to be close to twenty degrees. *Above* zero. Soft white clouds drifted overhead as Harry backed his sheriff's car down the cobblestone driveway, and headed out of Willmar, back toward Roseland.

"You have a wonderful wife, Sheriff," Bob said, looking over at Harry.

"One of a kind," Harry beamed.

"No," Bob replied. "No, she's not."

Harry looked over at him with a surprised look on his face, his beam eclipsed.

"I've got one just like her," Bob said with a big smile.

Harry returned Bob's smile. Harry had known they had something in common, the moment he laid eyes on him. Harry was sure that truly appreciating the love of a kind, generous woman in this day and age was rare. He was glad that Bob was one of the few.

Harry looked out his side window at the endless white terrain and reluctantly changed the subject. "The mother's not doing so good. She's got a lot of fluid in her lungs. They don't know if she'll make it. They want to air-lift her to North Memorial Hospital to see what they can do."

Bob nodded solemnly.

Harry continued, "The little girl — "

"Wendy," Bob interrupted.

"Wendy," Harry resumed, "Is just dehydrated and a little malnourished."

With a long face, Harry looked over at Bob and asked, "Did you know that she couldn't walk?"

Bob thought of the wheelchair he had seen in the minivan. His heart sank. "Yeah," he replied sadly.

"Brent—that's my deputy—got tied up with an accident on Highway 7 earlier this morning, so he didn't get out on the Luce Line Trail until nine or so. Brent found the sick woman's wallet under the driver's seat. She has a Rapid City, South Dakota, address on her expired driver's license. Her name is Roberta Carter."

Bob felt foolish. "Bernie and I never thought to look for any identification."

"That's alright, Bob," Harry said. "You boys were too busy trying to keep them alert and alive until the paramedics came." Harry's grin was reassuring. "Anyway," Harry resumed, "I got a hold of a woman at that address who gave me the number of another woman who used to be Roberta's landlady. The landlady said that Roberta and her little girl—Wendy—moved out about six months ago because they couldn't pay the rent. She heard that Roberta and her daughter were living in some kind of colony up in the Black Hills."

Bob shook his head sadly, thinking about how tough it must have been for Wendy. He asked, "Did Roberta have a husband? Where's the father of the little girl?"

Harry nodded, "That's a good question." He glanced over at Bob, and resumed telling the story, "The landlady said that Roberta's husband was killed about a year and a half ago. He was hit by a car in Deadwood, South Dakota. He was a welder by trade, but he also made large yard sculptures out of ornamental iron and sold them to tourists, to make some extra money. The landlady said that Wendy fell off one of her father's sculptures when she was eight years old. That's when she broke her back and lost the use of her legs."

Bob looked out the window of the cruiser, digesting the story. *How very sad for her*, he thought.

"The landlady said that Roberta's husband was never right after that. He kind of went nuts. He only showed up once in a while, and when he did, he ranted and raved about getting "'God's punishment.'" He said he was going to burn in hell for his wicked ways, and his sculptures were products of the devil." Harry looked over at Bob with a flat stare and resumed, "He was trying to get all of his sculptures back from the people he sold them to, to redeem his soul."

Bob looked back at Harry, dumbfounded. "That would be insane," Bob responded.

Harry nodded. "He'd been selling the sculptures for over twenty years."

Bob thought of something his high school history teacher once said to their class: *Human beings are capable of doing stranger things than words can properly describe.* That teacher was a World War II holocaust survivor.

"I went into the station and checked the wire before you got up," Harry continued. "A two-toned silver-and-black Ford Aerostar minivan was stolen from a handicraft store in Hill City, South Dakota, five days ago. The man who reported it stolen said that the thief might be a pretty, sandy-haired woman, about thirty years old. The woman might have a little girl with her." Harry smiled sadly at Bob. "The man in Hill City didn't file the report until yesterday, and if he gets the van back, he won't press charges."

Bob snickered, "That would explain how they got this far—if it's them."

Harry nodded in confirmation, and turned his car off County Road 5 onto the Luce Line Trail.

Bob looked into the grove of pine trees as they passed it. There was no sign of tents or any other activity. His friends would've concealed themselves well. They had been kicked off private property for camping before. Once in the middle of the night.

And I'm in a sheriff's car, Bob laughed to himself, *as a guest.*

They pulled up behind the deputy sheriff's cruiser. A tow truck was in front of that. The tow truck driver had dug out the snow in front of the minivan and was hooking up a cable to the front axle. The minivan looked like it was a two-tone Ford Aerostar.

Bob was amused at how simple it all looked in broad daylight.

Just another car stuck in a snow bank. It happened a thousand times on a typical Minnesota winter day.

Harry and Bob got out of the car and walked over to the deputy sheriff. He was a big man, built like the actor, Brian Dennehy. He looked like somebody that you didn't want to mess with. The deputy sheriff turned from looking at the minivan and smiled at the two newcomers, then he reported to Harry, "The van has a bunch of paintings in it. Landscape watercolors of the Black Hills. They're really somethin'. Maybe that's why the van was stolen."

Harry replied sharply, "We don't know that for sure. Did you leave the paintings in there?"

"Yeah," the deputy came back with a smirk. He liked to tease Harry. "I left everything inside."

The deputy sheriff extended his right hand to Bob with a sly grin on his face, "I'm Brent," he said.

The short, stocky man wearing knickers and a beard shook his hand. "Bob."

Brent rolled his eyes and said sarcastically, "I know. Everybody knows."

Bob laughed, but he felt strange doing it.

Brent thought, *Harry was right, when it comes to a handshake, I've met my match.*

Bob asked Brent, "Have you seen my friends?"

Brent nodded, "Roger Kendrick was here about an hour ago. He had two tall guys named Doug and John with him. They picked up another guy—about your size—named Bernie."

Brent's eyes sparkled mischievously, "Bernie stepped out of them pines back there. He must've been pickin' berries on my uncle's farm, I guess."

Bob looked at Brent sheepishly.

Brent patted his arm. "It's alright." Bob and Brent both laughed, but for different reasons.

The deputy continued, "Roger said that Dottie was making lunch at their place. You're supposed to join them when you can. That old fart made me drive to "71 and back around again so he could get out. If Earl had been here then," Brent hitched his thumb back at the tow truck driver, "I would've made him back up all the way to Roseland."

Brent's voice turned somber. He looked deeper into Bob's eyes and pulled a water bottle out of his jacket and said, "Bernie said to give this to you. He said you might need it this morning."

Bob was dumbfounded. He looked down at the amber-colored plastic water bottle, then back into Brent's cold eyes with embarrassment. Bob didn't know what to say.

Brent broke the awkward silence. "It's okay," he said, patting Bob's arm with a sad smile, "There ain't no law saying a guy can't have a drink if he wants one—even in front of a cop."

Bob looked down at the twelve-year-old Scotch in the plastic water bottle. It had been distilled the same year that his sister died. He unscrewed the cap and went to take a drink. He closed his eyes and thought about the wave of euphoria that would envelop his senses when the hot elixir flowed across his tongue, leading him into a dream world that nightmares are made of. He savored the thought of that moment as a child savors the thought of Christmas. Then he opened his eyes, and—for the first time in decades—he saw the bottle for what it really meant to him.

Bob poured the spirit on the blanket of perfect snow that lay about his feet and zipped the empty water bottle into his backpack.

The sheriff and his deputy looked on with silent reflection. Harry, then Brent, nodded in recognition to Bob's symbolic act, then turned and walked down the grade.

A shaft of light pierced a billowing cloud and illuminated the ice covering the south side of the minivan, as Earl used the tow truck's power winch to break it out of its' snowy prison. It took five minutes to pull it up onto the old railroad grade. All four of the men stood quietly watching the minivan like they were watching a bobber on a lake. It was covered in frost. The body heat inside of it for over two days had melted the snow on the outside, then the snow had refrozen, coating it like it was a glazed donut.

Harry scraped the snow off the back license plate. "South Dakota. A match," he said.

"I told you," Brent retorted, grinning at his boss. "But why is it on the Luce Line?"

Harry responded, "We don't know where she was going, but I'd guess that she was taking back roads to avoid being detected. The railroad grade probably looked like any other side road in the storm. She just drove off the edge in the blowing snow."

Bob piped up, "She might have been delirious from the flu, too," he said, recalling her condition.

The officers looked at him and nodded. They stood reflecting on their speculations for a minute or so while Earl was securing the minivan to the tow truck.

A crackling sound broke their concentration as it burst across the frozen landscape. The two-way radios in both cruisers were transmitting a call. Harry went back to his car, sat in his seat with the door open and keyed his microphone. Donna was calling.

Brent looked down the embankment at the hole in the snow where the van had just been. His eyes caught something shiny in the deep snow that had been trampled from all the activity. Brent half-walked, half-slid down the slope and picked up the object.

"A pearl-handled pocket knife!" Brent yelled up to Bob and Earl, holding it up to show them his find. Brent gave it a closer look and frowned. "Aw, but the blade's broken."

Brent was just about to toss the knife back in the snow when Bob yelled, "Wait! That's mine!"

Brent gave him a puzzled look, then his eyes twinkled. "Prove it," he shouted back.

"It's got my initials, 'BS' carved into the handle," Bob replied. He thought for a moment and added, "And 'AC,' next to it."

Brent looked closer at the pearl handles on the old knife. They were stained pink. He rubbed his thumb across one side of it. The roughly carved letters 'BS' and 'AC' appeared in blood.

"Well I'll be damned," Brent said, looking up at Bob. "Looks like you've got yourself a broken pocket knife! Who was 'AC'? A sweetheart or somethin'?"

Brent threw the knife, underhanded, up the grade. Bob caught it in his right hand. He looked down at it and grunted, "Something like that." Bob squeezed the knife hard for a few seconds and looked up at a small patch of cotton-ball clouds that were drifting slowly to the east. Then he zipped his lifelong companion into a side pocket of his jacket and suddenly got the urge to do something that he thought he would never want to do again. "Hey, Deputy!" he called out.

Brent looked up. He had been looking for more treasures in the snow.

"Is it okay if I take a look inside the van?" Bob asked him.

Brent looked over at Earl. "Does he have time?"

Earl replied in a voice tempered by a plug of tobacco in his lower lip. "He's got a minute."

Brent looked back at Bob, "I s'pose' it's okay. Just don't take nothin'." Brent chuckled under his breath. He had been inside that van. It wasn't likely anyone would want a souvenir from a place that smelled that bad.

Bob walked over to the passenger side of the minivan. The sun was starting to melt the frost off. The sliding door handle was exposed. Bob tugged on it. It gave an inch.

He tugged harder. It gave a lot of resistance, but it opened and slid all the way back.

The pungent odor hit Bob and the tow truck driver at the same time.

"Jesus!" Earl yelled, covering his nose with his forearm, "Did somebody die in there?"

It was a rhetorical question. Earl really didn't want the answer. He'd seen—and smelled—plenty of dead bodies in his day. It came with the job. Earl opened the driver's side door to give Bob some cross ventilation.

Bob climbed into the back of the minivan. It seemed to be a very different place than it was ten hours ago. For some reason it seemed smaller. Bob looked down and saw the corner of a photograph lying face down on the floor by the bench seat. The back of it was all faded and wrinkled, like it had been in the pocket of a pair of pants for a long time. Bob picked it up and turned it over. It contained the image of a pretty woman with light brown hair, a little blonde girl who was about six or seven, and a dark-haired man with a full beard and blue eyes—who bore a vague resemblance to himself.

"Daddy," Bob muttered to himself. "That's why she called me daddy."

Bob slid the photo into his jacket pocket.

He really was planning to give it to Harry, but he never did.

Bob raised his eyes to see a framed painting. It was of a deep blue lake with tan rock formations around it. Dark trees dotted the landscape. Variations in the color of shadows cast on the background snow brought it all together. It was captivating.

Bob flipped through to the next painting, then the next one, then the next, and so on. All of them were of different places, different seasons. All in the Black Hills of South Dakota. The use of light, color, and shadow was extraordinary. All the paintings were the same size, about two feet by three feet, and painted with watercolors on white cardboard.

These were facing the side of the van last night, he thought, *that's why I didn't see them.*

The deputy is the one who turned them around. Bob studied the first one closer. His eyes traveled across the scene until they got to the lower right hand corner.

The painting was signed by the artist: *wendy*

"What!?" Bob gasped, drawing back from the cardboard canvas.

In a daze, he slid the first painting to the left a few inches. It was signed the same. He repeated this ten more times. All of the paintings bore her name. Bob held his breath for a long minute, totally mesmerized as he immersed himself in the brush strokes that brought the scenes to life.

"She didn't make it."

Even though Bob was on his knees, he jumped about six inches. He took in a shallow breath and turned around to face Harry.

"She passed away about twenty minutes ago. I didn't mean to startle you," Harry said.

Harry was standing just outside the minivan's sliding door, his shoulders slumped as if he was carrying a very heavy weight. The news was a big letdown.

Bob snapped out of his trance. "Wendy?" he asked, his eyes probing and his voice cracking.

Harry caught the anguish on his face. "No," he replied painfully. "Her mother."

A wave of relief swept across Bob until he saw the grief in Harry's eyes.

"I'm so sorry," Bob said sadly. Bob felt like he was once again consoling his father after his sister died.

"We should have gotten here sooner."

Deputy Brent stepped into view. He was visibly shaken too. He looked at Bob with a sad curiosity. "Yeah, about that . . . how *did* you get here? How did you find the van?"

A hundred words flashed through Bob's mind, but the ones that came out were—"God's searchlights." Bob's voice was so soft, it was almost imperceptible.

"What?! What was that?" Brent asked.

"God's searchlights will lead us home," Bob said, quoting his great uncle, his voice a little louder.

Brent gave him a funny look, shook his head and walked away, saying disgustedly, "Ask a stupid question." About twenty feet down the grade, Brent turned around, looked at Bob, and said in a shaking, angry voice, "Weird city folks—who needs "em?"

Harry was still standing outside the door of the minivan. He was just as curious as Brent, and he *really* wanted to know what that statement meant, but he was sure that he would find out, sooner or later. All in due time. Harry was a patient man.

Bob redirected his focus and looked over at Harry. "Does Wendy know?" he asked Harry quietly.

"I don't know. She's with Social Services," Harry sounded more tired than Bob had seen him. "They can't find any family. Roberta's mother died years ago, and apparently her father was a drifter that she never really knew." Harry looked west, across the fields, in the direction of the Black Hills.

"The landlady said that Roberta was a loner. Likable, but not easy to make friends with."

"What will become of Wendy?" Bob asked sadly. His eyes were drawn back to the painting in front of him. The thought of her in some kind of foster home or orphanage was unbearable.

Harry took a deep breath. "I don't know how South Dakota handles it, but in Minnesota she'd become a ward of the state I suppose. Nobody wants a handicap—"

"I'm going to tell my wife that we should adopt her," Bob blurted out, looking back at the sheriff.

Harry looked at him soberly. "You'd do that?"

"We would," Bob replied, nodding his head.

"Are you sure that your wife would go for that?" Harry asked him solemnly.

Bob looked at Harry with a firm conviction. "She's just like Donna, remember?"

Harry responded with a smile that showed forty years of love and devotion.

Harry turned his watery eyes away from Bob and looked out across the snow-swept fields. "I remember," he said softly, then turned and walked slowly down the grade back to his cruiser.

Bob climbed out of the minivan. It was all set to go behind the tow truck.

Bob asked Earl, "Why can't you just get the van started and drive it the two miles to Blomkest? You wouldn't be on a road. It would never leave the trail."

Earl shook his head "no," and said, "Stolen. Liability, ya know."

Bob nodded. He was very familiar with liability. He owned a construction business.

Bob slammed the side door shut. The last sheet of ice and frost crashed to the old railroad grade, revealing the name of the handicraft store in Hill City where the minivan had been taken.

The name was stenciled on the side of the sliding door in large red letters, next to an outline drawing of "The Needles"— a rock formation in the Black Hills. The words read: "Art In Spires"

Bob laughed, recalling a game that he had played with his sister when they were kids.

Just add a word to make or change a sentence— and possibly its' meaning.

Art in-spires . . . Reflection.

Art in-spires . . . Compassion.

Art in-spires . . . Redemption.

The image of his Great Uncle standing in the doorway of the old log cabin came into focus in Bob's mind. He looked down at the Scotch stain in the snow and smiled. "And Uncle Art inspired salvation," Bob said under his breath.

He looked up at wispy clouds framed by a perfect blue sky. Somewhere out there, he just *knew* "the Wizard" was purring happily, pushing the big green boat across the water, carrying Uncle Art—and his sister—back to the bay to catch a batch of Pumpkinseed Sunfish.

Bob closed his eyes as a warm wave of peace and resolve blew through him like a freight train.

It was time he went fishing again.

He'd take his wife.

And Wendy.

And so it goes on . . .

Author's Notes

The fishing portions of this story, on Lake Trelipe, and Little Lake Hanging Horn, are drawn from true events—as well as I can remember.

The cross-country skiing portions on the Luce Line Trail from Gluek to Blomkest are based on a compilation of experiences that I had with friends on several separate ski trips on that desolate trail. On one of the ski trips, my friends and I found a late-model car buried in the snow along the Luce Line, but we didn't find anyone in it, so the overall story is still a work of fiction.

The characters in the story are based on bits and pieces of many people I've known over the years. That said, I was thinking of my friends, Doug Fries and John Liden, when I wrote this. Even though neither one of them has ever skied the Luce Line Trail, they both liked how I depicted them in the story.

The Bernie character, however, closely resembles a real man. On August 1, 2007, my good friend, Berndt Toivonen, went down on the Interstate 35W bridge collapse in Minneapolis. Despite his injuries, Bernie helped many people to safety, and he comforted a few more in their last mortal moments. His heroic and compassionate actions helped inspire part two of this story.

I skied the Luce Line trail for the first time in January of 1975, with Bernie and another friend, Steve Carmazon. This was promoted by the Minnesota Department of Natural Resources, as the first "rail to trail" conversion in the state of Minnesota. Steve set up the event. At the end of each day, Steve was to call in to Ralph Thornton, a journalist for the *Minneapolis Star and Tribune*. Mr. Thornton was assigned to write a compilation of our exploits in the newspaper over a several-day period. But, back in those days, communication broke down easily if you couldn't get to a pay phone on time—or if you lost your phone change in the snow—so our story ended up as a one-time blurb on a back page.

None of us were disappointed, though. We were just glad to be done skiing the trail after three long days. And, for several years after that, all of us went on to ski sections of the trail . . . together and with others.

The portion of the Luce Line Trail featured in this story, no longer exists. It has been reclaimed by the adjacent farms, and has vanished into the past like the buffalo that used to roam there. Only narrow, tree-lined remnants remain, in the now-quiet towns that it served.

For Bob Sorenson, everything came together under the vast open sky of the endless prairie: the past, present, future, and eternity.

We should all be so lucky.

I still have the pearl-handled pocket-knife — and the scar on the palm of my left hand. I cherish both.

I hope you liked the story, and if you did, tell one of your own. We are all full of stories.

It is how you will be best remembered.

ACKNOWLEDGMENTS

I would like to thank my high school creative writing teacher, Mrs. Beatrice Antholz, for encouraging me to write so long ago; my lovely wife, Barbara, for being patient and helping me through the torment; Christy Sauro, Jr.—the author of *The Twins Platoon*—for giving me the impetus to go on; the twenty nine "Victim Readers" (they know who they are) for allowing me to drag them through the process by reading my manuscript in various stages of development and giving me good, but sometimes painful advice; the staff at Mill City Press for helping me navigate through uncharted waters; my mom, who passed on to me a great love for the written word; and my Great Uncle Art, who not only gave me the best day of fishing I ever had, but also showed me that, for him, being physically handicapped was just a state of mind.